Wish you were here

COME WITH GETAWAY TOURS FOR EXCITING ADVENTURES IN THE MOST EXOTIC PLACES— IT'S THE ULTIMATE WAY TO SEE THE WORLD!

MEET THE GANG:

LUCI has always thought her life was so **normal**. She can't wait to travel, meet new people and experience different cultures—the tour is her dream come true!

JAY's mother is white and her father is black. Being different has made her strong and independent; she's the voice of reason to all the kids on the tour.

STACEY is the epitome of California glamour. Whether sitting in a bistro or touring a medieval castle, she's beautifully dressed, perfectly made-up—and ready to flirt.

DARIA thinks her wealthy rancher father sent her on the tour to punish her. She finds a friend in Stacey, who also has a powerful—and sometimes distant—father.

AIMEE's post—New Wave style and permanent headphones may give the impression that she's tuning out, but she's actually very smart and very tuned **in**.

GLIN is a long-haired guy from Vermont. Though his medieval wardrobe makes him stand out from the crowd, Luci thinks he's gorgeous **and** fascinating.

LOGAN is a man's man. He camps, climbs, flies, boats, and everything in between. His idea of love is a natural girl, so why is **Stacey** hitting on him?

FRANCINE ATKINSON is the Getaway tour guide. She's young, fun, adventurous, and best of all, she avoids tourist traps like the plague!

Don't miss:

Wish You Were Here: FRANCE
&
Wish You Were Here: NEW ORLEANS

(coming soon)

S0-DVC-123

Wish you were here:
IRELAND

ROBIN O'NEILL

B
BERKLEY BOOKS, NEW YORK

WISH YOU WERE HERE: IRELAND

A Berkley Book / published by arrangement with the author

PRINTING HISTORY
Berkley edition / August 1996

The Putnam Berkley World Wide Web site address is
http://www.berkley.com

ISBN: 0-425-15416-5

BERKLEY®
Berkley Books are published by The Berkley Publishing Group, 200 Madison Avenue, New York, New York 10016.
BERKLEY and the "B" design are trademarks belonging to Berkley Publishing Corporation.

PRINTED IN THE UNITED STATES OF AMERICA

10 9 8 7 6 5 4 3 2 1

To Jack and Virginia Leary
—there are never too many bullmastiffs

Acknowledgments

Ciarán O Braonáin, Enya Ní Bhraonáin,
Máire Ní Bhraonáin, Pol O Braonáin, Noel
O Dúgain, Pádraig O Dúgain
Randy, Happy
Fortune

Chapter One

"There's no railing!" Sixteen-year-old Luci McKennitt stopped dead in her tracks while everyone else on the Getaway Tour kept walking to the west.

One more inch and Logan Carlisle would be in the ocean. Leaning over the edge of the Cliffs of Moher as far as he possibly could, he watched the Atlantic crash onto the shore of western Ireland. "You can see straight down!"

"Logan, get away from the edge!" Fran Atkinson called out. Her voice was nearly lost in the wind.

He didn't move. "How far is it?"

"Six hundred and fifty-six feet," Fran replied as she took hold of his arm and pulled him back onto the plateau. "How will I explain it to your father if you're dashed to bits on the rocks below?"

Logan grinned. "Maybe I'll learn to fly on the way down."

"Give me strength, if you believe that," she replied.

Glin Woods was standing farther along the cliff. His long brown hair was streaming behind him. "Come on, Luci. You can do it." He held out his hand to her.

Luci shook her head.

There were a couple things she didn't like. Heights were definitely at the top of the list. Second was fast food, and really close spaces came in third. There was no risk of number two or three on this precipice, so all Luci had to do was avoid number one.

"Next time."

Jay Hamilton was standing near the edge. "It's beautiful, Luci. You can almost see America from here!"

"How far is America?" Daria Kenter asked.

"Three thousand miles. You just flew it," Stacey Rush replied impatiently.

"I slept the whole way," Daria grumbled.

"And you didn't wake up yet," Stacey commented.

The Aer Lingus flight had left John F. Kennedy International Airport in New York late the night before and had arrived at Shannon International Airport on the west coast of Ireland just after dawn. The jet had been painted green and white, the flight attendants had been dressed completely in green, and Luci had entertained fears that the food would be tinted green as well. It would have been a St. Patrick's Day celebration at thirty thousand feet.

But the flight had been uneventful and the landing without incident. No elves had appeared on the runway to prevent the jet from setting down. Fran, the tour guide, had informed them that when Shannon was being built, it had been necessary to import workers from England because no true Irish worker would disturb the fairy rings located on the site of the proposed runways.

The tourists had been amazed that in the modern world people could still believe in fairies, elves, and leprechauns, until Aimee Acacia explained that the Irish continued to live very close to the land and their ancient traditions. It was respect and reverence for these beliefs that caused the workers' refusal to disturb the unexplained circles in the earth.

Stacey had rolled her eyes. "Maybe you'll meet some leprechauns while you're there," she told Aimee.

"And wouldn't that be good luck," Aimee had answered with a smile.

Nothing ever seemed to disturb Aimee, who appeared to be the most good-natured person Luci had ever met. She still had her buzz-cut dyed black hair. The black nail polish was gone but the ever-present earphones remained.

While waiting to board the jet Luci couldn't help but ask to listen to the music to which Aimee seemed addicted. Aimee had passed her the cassette player and Luci adjusted the headset.

The music, if it could be called that, was a series of timeless tonalities that seemed to be playing in an echo chamber. There was nothing to hum, no words to sing.

Luci had handed the cassette player back to

Aimee with a shrug. "Theremin music must be an acquired taste," she said, which was the kindest thing she could think of.

Now seagulls whirled and cried in the air as the wind from the Atlantic whipped tears to Luci's eyes.

"These are the Cliffs of Moher. Aillte an Mhothair in Irish means the Cliffs of Ruin." Fran pointed to the south. "That's Hag's Head. It's named after a woman named Mal, who chased Cúchulainn all over Ireland."

"Cúchulainn was the Superman of Celtic tradition. He was more than Robin Hood and King Arthur combined," Glin added.

Fran smiled. "That's right. Mal fell to her death, Logan, off Loop Head, right into Galway Bay."

Logan turned away from the edge. "So she was clumsy. Can we walk along here?"

"I don't think so," Luci said under her breath.

"There's a path which goes to Aill Na Searrach, the Cliff of the Colts."

"Horses jumped off and died?" Daria grimaced.

"They were fairy horses," Fran replied.

"I don't know if that makes it any better," Daria commented.

"Why can't we go there?" Logan insisted.

"Because it rained last night and it will be slippery," Fran replied firmly.

"Does everything have to be an Iron Man contest for him?" Luci asked Jay, remembering their long bicycle ride at midnight and exploration of a cave in France. It had taken her days to recover.

Jay pulled an elastic from her pocket and fastened it around her hair. "Yes. Logan would probably dive right off the brink if someone suggested it. Cliff diving. Isn't that what it's called?"

"He wouldn't even need *Wide World of Sports*," Luci agreed.

"Is this all we're going to do on this trip? Stand and look?" Logan asked.

Fran shook her head. "No, I'm sure you'll find something to do that I'll wish you didn't."

Glin laughed.

Stacey pointed her toe. "I'm hardly wearing the kind of footwear compatible with hiking on a cliff."

"We told you to bring walking shoes," Logan informed her as he studied her delicate footwear.

"I did. They're packed."

"You should be wearing them," he replied.

"In the van? Why would I do that? We're not walking."

Fran held up her hand. "Enough! We've been in Ireland two hours and you're at it already. Any further clothing debates can be held in private. The rest of us are interested in the country. This is O'Brien's Tower." Fran pointed to the west. "Out there are the Aran Islands. There are three islands— Inishmore, Inishmaan, and Inisheer."

Stacey gazed into the distance. "That's where the sweaters come from."

Clothing again.

Luci shook her head. Stacey could diminish the most breathtaking view by transforming it into a shopping excursion.

"That's right, Stacey," Fran responded patiently. "Every family had their own intricate pattern."

"That's so when the fishermen wash up on the stone, they can identify the bodies," Glin said.

"Be serious!" Stacey retorted.

Fran nodded. "That's true."

Daria shrugged. "I still want to get a couple. They make good presents."

"You'll never be able to wear them in California; they're very heavy," Jay pointed out. "I wore one when I lived in Montreal and I didn't have to wear a coat on top of it."

"So what? The point is giving someone a present, not if they ever use it."

Luci and Jay exchanged a glance. Daria had a different sense of money than either of them did.

Daria and Stacey seemed to have virtually unlimited spending money. They purchased whatever took their fancy. Neither Jay nor Luci had a budget for such folly and it did matter to them if their gifts were useful and appreciated.

In fact, if it hadn't been for Luci picking up a coin in a cave in France, neither she nor Jay nor Glin nor Logan would have been in Ireland right then. That coin, which she had believed was a quarter Glin had thrown down to mark their path, had proven to be a Roman coin dating from 200 A.D., during the reign of the Emperor Septimus.

The finders' fee had been remarkably generous and they had split it evenly, four ways, to ensure that they would be able to travel together for a long time.

Luci's parents had put most of the money in a secure investment for her college education. Knowing how much she loved to travel, they had nevertheless agreed that she could use a portion to satisfy her wanderlust.

The money had been a blessing for Jay, who had recently moved to Westport, Connecticut, from Montreal, with her single mother. Money was very tight in her family and this was an enormous help.

"What are we going to do at this hotel?" Daria asked as they walked back to the van.

"There is a lovely river. You could fish. Logan might try going after the trout with his bare hands, but the rest of you probably want to use rods and reels." Fran winked at Logan. "And there's pony trekking, of course."

Jay walked a bit faster to catch up with Fran. "I'm glad you brought that up. I don't know that much about riding."

"There are horses for all levels. I think most of it will be restricted to the bridle paths around Connemara. It's pretty safe."

"So what fun is that?" Logan jumped in.

"What's wrong with just walking and admiring the scenery?" Luci asked.

"It's bor-ing," Logan said.

"You can go on a roundup or something," Fran replied. "Just wear a helmet!"

They reached the parking lot and Fran opened the door to the van. "He'll be wanting to hang glide off the Twelve Bens. I'll be shipping him home in itsy-bitsy little vials."

"Don't count on it," Logan said as he got in the van.

Jay paused. "I think I'd like to go to the . . ."

"Hmmm. Me, too," Luci agreed, seeing the look her friend shot her.

Fran pointed.

The two girls headed toward the comfort facilities.

"What's the deal with you and Glin?" Jay asked when they were alone.

"There's no deal," Luci said.

"You've hardly said ten words to him since New York."

Luci sighed. It was true. She didn't know what to say to Glin. After the trip to France they had kept in contact by computer. E-mail proved to be perfect. It was instantaneous communication and . . . well, silent. Luci could take time to plan exactly what she was going to say.

She didn't want to say the wrong things to Glin. They seemed to be friends and that's how it was all going along. He never made a suggestion that the relationship could be anything else.

"But you really like him," Jay continued.

"That's true."

"He kissed you in France!"

"So? Are you going to make a major issue of that?"

"Are you trying to tell me that didn't mean anything?"

"I'm not sure it did."

"Luci, I could strangle you," Jay said as she walked into the building.

"Why?"

"What if you're giving him the impression that you don't like him because you're acting so aloof?"

Jay closed the door to the stall.

"Oh, put the pressure on me, why don't you?" Luci said to the door.

"It's not me," Jay replied.

Luci leaned against a sink. "What am I supposed to do?"

Jay opened the door and went to wash her hands. "Act like yourself. I've seen you a dozen times since France and you've never acted like a stiff with me. Why do it with him?"

"I don't know! Because I want him to like me."

"You don't want me to like you?"

"Of course!"

"What's the difference?" Jay asked.

Luci thought about it. "No difference?"

"None. I like you as you are usually. You're not the usual you with Glin. Are you doing him a favor?"

"No."

"So stop!" Jay laughed as she linked her arm through Luci's. "If he doesn't like you as you are, kick him to the curb!"

Luci laughed as they headed back to the van. "He *is* cute, isn't he?"

"Beautiful."

"Do you really think so?"

"Absolutely. He's got great eyes."

Glin was standing alongside the van as they approached, looking every bit as good as Luci remembered.

Sometimes she thought she was making him up. She'd be typing at the computer, imagining him at his computer in Vermont, and she'd almost convince herself that he couldn't possibly be as attractive, as nice, or as smart as she remembered.

Luci wondered if it had to do with being on her first European trip and the excitement of looking for a lost treasure; everything had seemed new and seemingly larger than life. She thought she could have deluded herself about Glin, too.

When she saw him in the waiting area of the airport, though, Luci knew it wasn't a fantasy. He was one hundred percent real.

Jay got into the van first. Luci knew her friend had done that on purpose so she'd have to sit next to Glin for the next leg of the trip.

He held out his hand. Luci put her hand in his and sat down. Glin sat down next to her.

"How do you like Ireland so far?"

"It doesn't look like any of the pictures I've ever seen," Luci admitted. "I expected lush green fields and rolling hills."

"That's farther to the east," Fran interjected. "The west coast is much more of a study in contrasts. Further up the road we'll be going through the Burren. Land doesn't come much rockier than that," she pointed out. "Boireann means rocky place in Irish."

"I thought the language was called Gaelic," Luci said.

"Technically, Gaelic refers to several dialects spoken both in and out of Ireland, while Irish refers only to the language in Ireland. In the language, there is no distinction. It's Gaeilge."

Jay looked out the window at several cows making their way along the large and craggy mountains. The sky was fifty shades of gray and the mist was so heavy it might as well have been called rain.

"Do you speak Irish?" Luci asked.

"Enough to get by. I lived here for a summer while I was in college. We were excavating the remains of early and medieval churches on the Aran Islands. I lived in a house in Kilronan on Inishmore."

"That must have been fascinating," Glin admitted.

"It was a wonderful experience. Of course, it made me give up my dreams of being an archaeologist." Fran laughed.

"Why?" Jay asked.

"Because I became more interested in seeing how people lived than in digging in the dirt. As much as you can learn about a culture from the kind of pots they used, I wanted to look up instead of down. Just a personal quirk, I guess."

Stacey and Daria, who had also decided to use the facilities, arrived back at the van.

"Logan's up on the side of the cliff," Stacey said as she settled in.

Fran put her head down on the steering wheel.

Chapter Two

"**I**t's nothing but rocks," Daria observed as they stood on a hillside.

This was the Burren. All around them were rocks. Beyond the rocks were stone walls six feet high made of more rocks. Someone, long ago, had attempted to create pastures from what looked like a moonscape.

"Over there. Tourists! May I have your attention? Thank you. Those are granite erratics left on the limestone by the departing glaciers in the Ice Age. Date, please?"

"A hundred years ago?" Logan teased.

"Times ten thousand," Glin replied.

"Right. About one and a half million years ago," Fran said.

Stacey nudged a rock with her foot. "This is valuable?"

"That's what Oliver Cromwell's English soldiers said when they got here. Too few trees to hang anyone on, too little water to drown anyone in, and too little earth to bury them in," Fran replied.

Glin held out his hand. "But, hey, we come in peace!"

Fran nodded. "It's true, Cromwell is not a popular figure to the Irish. He destroyed a great deal more than he created. The countryside is littered with ruins caused by his soldiers."

"I'll bet there are some pretty interesting caves around here." Logan got down on his knees to follow a small stream as it disappeared into the folds of the rock strata.

"No more caves!" Luci and Jay replied simultaneously.

Logan shook his head.

"We have a choice to make, tourists. We can go to Corcomroe Abbey, which is close, or continue on to Connemara."

"What's at the abbey?" Stacey asked as she delicately picked her way between the rocks.

"Technically, it's a ruin."

"Terrific." Stacey was unimpressed.

"A very nice one," Fran continued. "It has a Cistercian house founded in 1180. Most of it is still standing."

"Most, huh?" Stacey said. "What's the fascination with ruins? Isn't there anything new to see?"

Luci began heading back to the van, determined not to slip on the wet rocks or plop herself into the mud. She wanted to maintain at least an illusion of dignity.

"I'm hungry," Daria said.

"Is this a really great ruin or will there be a similar ruin farther along?" Jay asked.

Fran smiled. "You're talking to someone who had dreams of being an archaeologist, so all ruins are great ruins to me, but I'm sure you will never regret passing this one up. If you're hungry, we can find some pub grub along the way."

Reaching the van, Stacey lost no time in scraping off the bottoms of her shoes. "Sounds delicious. Ugh."

"Pub grub is simple but good."

"Is it fried?"

In France, Stacey had eaten salads, not even trying the cheese or pastries. Everyone else had sampled the regional foods and enjoyed it. Luci was looking forward to doing the same here.

"What's a pub?" Daria asked.

Glin sat down next to Luci and Logan squeezed in next to Jay, so there were four in a seat that held three. Luci looked questioningly across the van to Logan. He gazed at Stacey, who was busily wiping off her shoes with a tissue.

"A pub is a public house, a bar," Fran said.

"We're not allowed in bars," Stacey said dubiously.

"This is not America and you're not drinking. It's a restaurant, trust me," Fran replied. "They serve sandwiches, soups, maybe a hot plate of roast beef or chicken."

"Salad?" Stacey asked.

"I doubt it."

"What about greens?"

"We'll tether you outside and you can graze on the grass," Logan teased as he pushed his damp hair off his face.

"Maybe we can stop at a supermarket . . ." Luci began.

"We stopped at every Monoprix in France," Stacey shot back. "We're not doing that here!"

"You can get your own salad there," Luci pointed out.

Jay's guidebook was open. "The Quinnsworth is the supermarket chain in Ireland."

"Cool. We can stop, right?"

"You're a sociologist after my own heart, Luci, my dear," Fran answered as she drove back to the road.

Glin couldn't have been any closer to Luci. Her hipbone was jammed against the door and still there wasn't a millimeter of spare space. The van bumped over a rut and they were jostled still closer together.

It was going to be a long ride to Connemara.

"Oughterard is called the gateway to Connemara," Fran remarked as they drove along the main road out of Galway. The landscape was becoming more gentle; there were long expanses of green pastures and trees along the fence lines.

"It's a very popular tourist destination because of Lough Corrib, which is the largest lake in the Republic of Ireland. Anglers fish for salmon and trout. We missed the biggest annual event, though."

"Which is?" Luci asked.

"Every year in May the gnats hatch and the lake

swarms with these delectable bugs. It's a true feeding frenzy for both the fish and the fishermen."

"Gnats bite," Stacey commented. "I'm allergic to them."

"Not to worry, Stacey, the gnat season has passed," Fran said.

"If you let them bite you enough, you build up an immunity," Logan told her.

"What a good suggestion. I could get red and puffy waiting for that to happen," Stacey snapped.

"You know, when you get too far away from the real world, you should expect to get weak," Logan said.

"Allergies are weaknesses?" Stacey shot back.

"Sure," Logan replied.

Fran waved her hand. "No medical debates."

Logan was going to be reasonable. "Fran, you know what it's like to sleep outside on the rocks. It makes you tough. It makes you strong. You eat some dirt and you stop getting sick. You can't sterilize the entire world."

Luci put her hand over her eyes.

For a fair amount of his life Logan had been raised under very rough conditions on his grandparents' ranch in Montana. This led him to expect that everyone would be as sturdy as he was. Anyone was in danger of being considered a wimp if they wanted to sleep in a bed or at least a bedroll.

But Logan was also charming and Luci admired him. He had a spirit that wouldn't quit and was fearless as well as loyal. He made everyone do more than they thought they could.

Eating dirt was out of the question, though.

Logan persisted. "What's a vaccine? The same disease in a milder dose. If you roll in poison ivy, you acquire an immunity to it. It's medical science."

"If I rolled in poison ivy, I'd get big welts all over my body," Jay declared.

Aimee smiled. "You should ask why you need illness."

Everyone turned to her.

"What do you get from your allergies, Stacey?" Aimee continued.

Logan stifled a laugh.

"I don't *get* anything. I *get* sick."

"The possibility exists that you want to get sick. Maybe you want to avoid something. Maybe you want attention. Maybe you want a couple days off to feel sorry for yourself."

Luci lowered her head and prayed Jay would be able to control herself. One little gasp of laughter, and Luci would be done for.

"I don't feel sorry for myself," Stacey snapped.

Aimee smiled. "I'm sure you'll find the reason someday."

"Where'd you hear this medical bulletin?" Stacey asked.

"My mother. Once you understand the three bodies—"

"Three bodies?" Glin asked.

Please, Luci begged silently. Don't ask!

"The etheric, the physical, and the mental, then you will understand illness."

The sun was just beginning to come out from

behind the clouds as they arrived in front of the Corrib pub.

Fran pulled the key out of the ignition. "Let's take our physical bodies into the pub and feed them, and let our other bodies get along as best as they can without us."

"Sounds good to me," Logan replied.

Jay got out and admired the view. "This is beautiful!"

Lough Corrib rested at the bottom of the valley and the surrounding hillsides were dotted with grazing cows.

"It's possible to take a boat to an island in the lake called Inchagoill, which means Island of the Foreigner. There are the remains of two churches. . . ."

Stacey groaned.

Fran ignored her and continued. "One is from the fifth century, tourists. That's fifteen hundred years ago."

Daria shrugged.

Fran walked toward the pub. "The other church is from the twelfth century and has been restored."

"Will we be distraught if we miss those?" Jay asked.

"Seeing the enthusiasm generated so far, I doubt it."

"Aren't there churches by the side of the road we can just look at from the van?" Stacey asked.

"Okay. We don't go to Inchagoill. Let me tell you what's there because it's significant. There's an obelisk with grafitti on it. Of course, the carving is in Latin. It may be the oldest inscription in Latin anywhere in Europe outside of Rome."

Glin nodded, the only one riveted by the information.

Fran sighed. "Why don't you just tell me what you want to see and we'll go do that?"

Luci laughed. "Fran, we've never been here before. We have to rely on your good judgment!"

"I see how heavily you depend on my advice." She smiled.

Glin opened the door to the pub and they went inside.

There was a bar to the left of the entrance, the wall behind it lined with tankards and unusually shaped bottles. A dartboard was prominently displayed on the far wall. To the right was a dining area with large windows facing the lake.

A woman hurried from the bar and disappeared into the kitchen. "Find yourselves a seat. I'll be right with you."

The group pulled two tables together and arranged the seats quickly.

"I want to look at the lake."

"I want to look at the street."

"I want to face the pub."

Aimee smiled. Fran reached over and removed her earphones. "Aren't those batteries ever going to die?"

"If you bury them once a month during the full moon, they recharge," Aimee replied.

Luci couldn't tell if Aimee was being serious or not, and no one had the courage to ask. Stacey had her compact out and was checking her hair in the mirror.

"Is it this damp every day? Look at this frizz."

"This is the west coast of Ireland. You can count on rain six days out of seven," Fran replied.

"You're kidding."

"No."

Stacey snapped the compact shut. "So. What kind of grubs do they serve here?"

Jay choked and coughed.

"Ugh," Daria moaned.

"There's nothing wrong with eating grubs," Logan asserted. "Had them in Australia. They only look squishy."

Stacey glared at Luci. "What does the Brutal Gourmet say? Grubs taste just like chicken?"

Luci paused for a moment. "They do if you sauté them in olive oil and lemon juice. And don't forget the capers."

Everyone was laughing as the hostess came to the table. "That's what I like, happy patrons. What can I get you?"

"Where's the menu?" Stacey asked.

"There are the specials of the day, one hot, one cold. And soup."

Luci smiled. "It keeps things simple."

The hostess chuckled. "That it does."

They made their choices and the hostess left.

"What do you want to do while you're here?" Fran asked.

Logan leaned back in his chair and balanced it

precariously on two legs. "I want to do some fly-fishing."

"I want to ride," Daria said.

"You have six horses at home," Stacey commented.

"I'd like to hear some traditional Irish music," Glin offered.

Fran turned to Luci. "You want to go to the supermarket and what else?"

"Am I that predictable?" Luci asked.

"Yes," they answered in concert.

Logan glanced at Jay. "We haven't heard from you. Put your two cents in before it's too late."

"I'd like to see some of the Irish crafts—the knotwork, the woolens, the illuminations," Jay replied.

"I think all of that can be arranged," Fran assured them. "We'll be in Ballynahinch in a couple hours. If you want, there will be enough time to ride. Or fish, I suppose. The MacNeasas will be glad help you do whatever you want." Siobhan and Liam MacNeasa were old friends of Fran's who had just opened an inn.

The hostess returned with a tray holding bowls of soup. "It's potato mushroom today you'll be having."

Luci could smell the aroma of the fresh soup wafting from the bowl. "It looks delicious."

Stacey stared at her bowl. "What's this in it?" She pointed to a swirl of white.

"Cream, dear."

Luci stirred the heavy cream into the soup and took a spoonful. "Heavenly."

"Thank you," the hostess replied, and departed.

"How can you?" Stacey asked.

"I'm hungry," Luci answered.

Stacey attempted to scoop the cream out and put it on her bread plate.

Jay glanced over to Luci and shook her head.

Glin broke a slice of soda bread in half and offered a piece to Luci. "Fran, have you been to River House before?"

"Yes. It's a beautiful spot, right on the river. The house was a hunting lodge for many years, then about a year ago my friend Siobhan and her husband Liam bought it. They've spent months modernizing the kitchen, restoring another section, replanting the gardens. There's a stable."

"A spa?" Stacey asked. "An exercise room? A pool?"

"No. It was simply a hunting lodge."

"You could sit on the bank of the river and dunk your feet," Daria suggested.

"Don't tell her to do that," Logan interjected. "She'll scare all the fish."

"It sounds dull. I hope we're not going to get stuck there," Stacey grumbled.

"You won't be disappointed," Fran assured her.

The hostess put enormous sandwiches in front of them.

"What do you do for entertainment?" Stacey asked.

"Siobhan says there's a ghost."

Stacey lifted the top of her sandwich and began scraping the mayonnaise off the bread. "Oh, that should be great fun."

Chapter Three

Connemara was a Gaeltacht region, a part of Galway where Irish was considered the primary language. All the road signs appeared with the Irish first and English below. It was barren, though not as rocky as the Burren. Outside of Oughterard they drove past the Maumturk Mountains. Sheep, cows, and donkeys ate freely of the available grass, with no fences to keep them off the road. There were no towns and few houses. What houses existed were often stone cottages.

"Welcome to beautiful downtown Recess," Fran commented as they drove through a village of fewer than a dozen buildings.

Luci turned in her seat to get a better look as the town receded behind them. "It's bigger than Maam Cross."

"Four corners in the middle of nowhere," Stacey observed.

"And remarkable corners they were," Glin replied.

Logan was undaunted. "I think it's outstanding. What's the chance we can camp out in those mountains?"

Luci hadn't flown three thousand miles to camp out in the mist on hard ground and cook campfire stew. She wanted to sleep in a beautiful room with a comfortable bed and hot and cold running water. Those arrangements were made. They were staying at River House. It wasn't likely she was going to give that up without a severe fight.

"Slim to none," Fran replied, turning off the main road.

"Figures."

Luci breathed a sigh of relief, knowing that Logan was thinking they were a bunch of soft blobs. Except for Glin, who as Logan's best friend was exempt from disapproval.

"We'll go fishing," Glin assured Logan.

Daria was surprised. "Don't you want to go riding?"

"Pony trekking?" Logan asked, saying each word clearly and dripping with disdain.

"You agreed to come on this trip!" Luci reminded him.

Jay nodded. "You said it sounded like fun."

"There are things available to us that do sound like fun, but everyone seems determined to avoid them at all costs."

Glin held up his hands. "This is not a problem. There are twenty-four hours in every day; I'm sure we'll be able to do something for everyone. Let's not waste time arguing."

"Thank you, Glin," Fran said. "Look, we're coming up to the town of Ballynahinch."

It was by far the largest village they had seen in the last hour or so. A town square was at the center with buildings surrounding it. There were several shops, a grocery store, a hardware store, and a post office in addition to town houses.

"What's going on up ahead?" Jay asked.

There were about ten people gathered in front of a pub. As they approached, Fran slowed the van. Then it was possible to read the signs the people were holding.

NO MORE HUNTING.
STOP CRUELTY TO ANIMALS.
BLAZERS GO TO BLAZES.
THE UNSPEAKABLE IN PURSUIT OF THE UNEATABLE.

Luci stared at the protesters in amazement. "Picketing in this tiny town?"

"What are they protesting?" Daria asked.

Fran continued down the road. "It seems they're protesting the local foxhunt, the Connemara Blazers."

"Why?" Daria asked.

"Animal rights," Logan said. "With no respect for natural balance."

"Enough," Fran announced. "We're here now, let's enjoy ourselves, not get into a discussion of what's politically or ecologically correct. Can you do that for me?"

Logan nodded as they continued through town.

The road narrowed and wound its way into a wooded area. Soon the van went through a gateway and down a long pebble driveway. As they swung around a corner River House came into view.

It was a very large brownstone house, three stories tall in the middle with a wing sprawling out to the right. The middle section appeared to be the oldest, as the architecture was more intricate.

Fran parked to the side and they all stepped out of the van. In a moment a young, slim woman opened the front door and hurried down the steps.

"Fran!"

"Siobhan!"

The two women exchanged hugs.

"You made it!"

"It wasn't easy," Fran teased, looking toward the others.

"You're our first guests," Siobhan told them. "We should have had more of a celebration to welcome you here."

Stacey groaned. "They have to practice on us?" she asked under her breath.

A large man stepped outside. "Fran! Good to see you!"

"Liam!" Fran went up the stairs and was nearly lost in the hug of this bearlike man.

Luci and Jay followed Fran up the granite steps and went through the large wooden doors. The foyer was warm and inviting and Luci knew she'd be very happy staying there.

Stacey entered the house carrying her duffel bag. Suddenly there was a sharp bark, followed by a howl. A small white-and-brown beagle came scampering down the hall and pushed her way into the crowd. She leaped on Stacey's leg, clawing for a foothold so she could climb.

Stacey jumped back. "Get down!"

"Tess!" Siobhan ordered sharply. "Sit! Down! Stay!"

The puppy didn't listen. The more Stacey backed away, the more the dog followed as though it were a game.

"Maybe it's your perfume," Jay offered, holding back her laughter.

Siobhan scooped Tess into her arms. "Tess doesn't have any manners yet, but she's only sixteen weeks old."

"She looks like a quick study," Stacey commented dryly.

Liam had his arms full of suitcases and bags. "Let's get you settled into your rooms. Then we can have a walk around the grounds before dinner."

Tess squirmed and struggled in Siobhan's arms, yapping as the group went past.

"She's just excited by all the new faces," Fran remarked.

"She wasn't looking at my face," Stacey asserted as she trailed Liam up the main staircase.

Luci was about to follow when Siobhan stopped her.

"There's a lovely room in the new wing. It's right on the river. Maybe you'd like it."

"Sounds terrific," Jay admitted.

Siobhan put Tess back on the floor. "Come along, then, and I'll show it to you."

Luci and Jay went with Siobhan along a hallway and down some stairs.

"This wing was built early this century for guests. It gave the family privacy, as well as the visitors," Siobhan explained.

"Fran told us this was a hunting lodge. It's huge."

"Over the three hundred years it's existed, it's been many things, and grown larger with age. I don't expect we'll be doing any building while we own it. It was quite a mess when we bought it, but we've gotten it into shape."

"I'd say so," Luci agreed.

Siobhan opened the door and they stepped inside the room.

It was perfect. There were sliding-glass doors along the back wall that opened out onto the lawn. Beyond that was the river and mountains.

"If you'd like to be in the older part of the house, you have a choice of rooms, but this is one of my favorites."

"Oh no, I love it here, don't you, Jay?"

"It's fantastic. How could anything be better?"

Siobhan smiled. "I'm glad to hear that. If there's anything you need, there are phones in all the rooms. I can't guarantee they always work, as we're still testing all the systems, but you can try calling."

Luci put her bag down. "I don't think we'll need anything."

"Wonderful. We'll meet in the garden in about an

hour and have a tour of the place," Siobhan said, and left.

Jay sat in an overstuffed armchair. "This is gorgeous."

Luci went to the window and watched the river flow by. "I hope everyone else enjoys it."

"You mean Logan?"

Luci nodded. "The agreement was that we'd decide on the trips as a group. We talked about coming here. Now he doesn't seem . . ."

"Happy here?"

"Does he?"

"He's looking for a challenge. Once he finds it, he'll settle down."

"I don't want to be compelled to go white-water rafting on every trip just because Logan wants excitement."

Jay twisted her hair into a knot on the top of her head. "I think it'll be okay. If it's not, we'll gang up on him and beat him with a shamrock until he behaves. Stop worrying."

"You're right. Logan can take care of himself." Luci unzipped her bag and began unpacking the necessaries.

An hour later they all strolled to the stable.

"We have twenty horses, from the most placid baby-sitter to some youngsters who are just learning their lessons, and one—" Liam began.

"One who should be sold," Siobhan finished.

"Balar has a good heart."

"And four flashing hooves," Siobhan replied.

"What's his deal?" Logan asked.

Jay raised her eyebrows at Luci.

"He's a hell-raiser," Siobhan replied. "I'm terrified of him and I've been riding my whole life."

Logan smiled. "He sounds like fun."

Liam gave Logan a firm pat on the back. "He's all yours, my boy. Want to ride him now?"

"Sure!" Logan beamed.

"Case closed," Jay whispered to Luci.

"Who else would like to ride this afternoon?"

Daria raised her hand. No one else moved.

"I think traveling wears some of us out," Fran explained.

Luci didn't feel worn-out, she just wasn't sure she wanted to jump on a strange horse and head out over the hills with Logan in the lead. Her experience on horseback had been confined to summer camp, which hadn't prepared her for anything outside of a confined area. They had taken one trail ride, but it had been strictly walking. Luci didn't suppose walking was the speed Logan had in mind.

"I'd like some tea," Siobhan said. "It's about that time of day for me."

"That would be lovely," Fran agreed as they began walking back to the house.

Daria rushed on ahead to get her riding gear while Logan helped Liam with the horses.

Twenty minutes later they were carrying trays of tea, cups, and biscuits to a table on the terrace. Fran poured while Siobhan served.

She held out a plate of cookies to Stacey. "Would you like a biscuit?"

Stacey looked down with some confusion.

Fran laughed. "Cookies, Stacey. Different word, same butterfat content."

"No, thank you," Stacey replied.

There was the sound of hoofbeats on the driveway.

"Hang on there, lad!" Liam shouted.

Luci turned her head.

Logan was riding a dark horse who was prancing down the driveway, rearing on his two hind legs.

"No problem!" Logan called back. "I've got him!"

Daria's horse bucked, then they all plunged out of sight behind some large rhododendrons.

"Logan's happy now," Jay commented.

"Afraid so," Fran replied.

Siobhan held out the biscuits to Luci. "You're probably used to more exotic fare," she admitted. "The Irish tend to simple food well prepared. Fancy foods seem too continental. I think being an island people, we like to keep our independence. We've certainly had our share of uninvited visitors."

"The English," Luci said.

"Oh yes. But they were hardly the first. There were native people already here when the Celts came around 300 B.C. Then there were the Norsemen in 785 A.D. and the Normans around 1170."

Glin took a biscuit. "Some of the Irish have very dark hair. Some have red with freckles."

Siobhan smiled. "The black Irish." She patted her dark hair. "We're the originals. We like to say we were here first. Some historians say those were Pictish people. Very old inhabitants. The Irish with red hair are of Norse lineage."

Fran took a sip of her tea. "There are historical records that say the Celts were quite tall, over six feet, with long hair that they smeared with lime to make white, and they fought naked. Both men and women were very fierce. Everyone in Europe was afraid of them."

Siobhan smiled broadly. "And rightfully so."

"Doesn't legend tell us the original inhabitants were the Fomorians?"

Siobhan grinned. "We have a scholar."

"Glin is that and more," Fran agreed.

Siobhan settled into her chair. "Every group of people has its version of the history of the world. The Celts in Ireland were no exception. To them, the Fomorians were demons. They were followed by the Tuatha De Dananns, another supernatural race but very human."

Aimee smiled. "There were the Druids."

"The spooks with the long cloaks?" Stacey asked.

"No one really knows what the Druids wore or what they believed," Siobhan admitted. "Though they have captured everyone's imagination."

"They were shamans," Glin said.

"Which are?" Jay asked.

"Spiritual advisers. Medicine men. Wisewomen," Aimee replied.

Again Luci was surprised by what Aimee seemed to know.

"Lots of people claim to be Druids today. You see them at Stonehenge."

Glin laughed. "You see them in Brattleboro."

"And Sedona," Aimee agreed. That was where she lived in Arizona.

"I don't believe in any of that baloney," Stacey said.

"Neither do I," Aimee said with a straight face.

Luci couldn't decide if Aimee was kidding or not.

Fran and Siobhan caught up on the latest news and gossip while the others finished their tea.

As Luci put her cup down on the table, Glin looked over to her. "Want to take a walk by the river?"

Luci's mind ground to a halt and she glanced at Jay.

"Not me," Jay said. "I'm going to rest before dinner."

Luci turned back to Glin. Was she really going to be alone with him?

"Go along," Fran encouraged them. "We've got a while before dinner. But give me a break. Don't get lost."

"We'll follow the river, that way we can't go wrong," Glin said as they went down the slight incline to the water.

The sun had already set behind the mountains as they reached the river. The banks were a few feet from the water, and as they left the area immediately near the house, tall grasses replaced the manicured lawn.

There was no sound but the water rippling over the large rocks. It was so unlike Luci's home in Manhattan, where even though she could walk through Central Park, there was always the roar of traffic in the background.

"This must be like your home," Luci said.

"Quite a bit," Glin answered. "We live about fifteen minutes from town, at the end of a dirt road. It's fairly remote. We're more on top of the mountain than in a valley."

"Do you like being so far away from everything?" Luci tried to imagine living in the country, where the nearest store might be twenty miles away. There would be good things about it, but she could envision problems, too. It would be a difficult transition for her.

"That's where I've always lived. I know there are kids at school who can't wait to go to college in a city, Boston or Baltimore, but I can wait. I've been to cities. I've seen what's there. I don't think I'm missing too much."

"But you do travel."

"That's true."

Glin often traveled with his father, who was a musician and played small concerts around the country. Also, Logan's father, who was a pilot, picked Glin up at a local Vermont airport whenever possible so he and Logan could spend weekends together in Atlanta or Montana.

The terrain became rougher with brush and brambles tangling the path. Glin stopped, turned to

Luci, put his finger to his lips, and pointed. There were two small deer grazing near the river. They picked up their heads and faced the humans. A moment later they had turned and bounded away, their white tails disappearing into the undergrowth.

"How beautiful they are. How graceful," Luci said, sitting on a nearby boulder. "You must live with sights like that every day."

Glin nodded. "Every day."

"How did you know so much about . . . who was it, the Fomor . . . Femur . . ."

"Fomorians. I was raised with the mythology of many countries. They were my comic books."

Glin's mother was a professor of medieval studies at an exclusive college in Vermont. Luci imagined their house must have been full of rare books and half-forgotten stories.

"Every country has tales of great warriors, courageous kings, and—"

"Beautiful, passive ladies," Luci finished for him.

Glin grinned. "Hardly. The Celts have a tradition of strong women, queens who ruled well and fought bravely."

"Just stories."

"Boadicea is hardly an invention. She fought the Romans and her chariot had great scythes on the wheels."

"Sort of like a James Bond device?"

"Exactly. At least that's how she's portrayed. The Celtic women were equals to the men. They had all kinds of rights under the law. Up until the conversions to Christianity, there were goddesses the men worshiped right alongside the women."

Glin paused.

"What?" Luci asked.

"It seemed like you've been avoiding me for the last twenty-four hours."

"How far could I get?" asked Luci, a little surprised at the sudden shift in topic.

"Not in actual distance, maybe, but . . ."

How could she explain this without seeming like an idiot?

"We've spent a lot of time sending mail back and forth."

"On the computer!" Luci replied.

"What's the difference?"

"I could think first about what I was going to say. When I'm with you . . . I could say something . . . without thinking and then you would think . . . I'm not sure what you would think, but I wouldn't want you thinking the wrong thing!"

Glin grinned. "Oh! That explains it!"

Luci groaned. "I didn't say that well. See?"

"You don't need to analyze everything you say before you say it. Just say something!"

"I don't have much experience with this."

"Me neither."

"Am I supposed to believe that?"

"Yes."

"It seems so impossible that you aren't surrounded or haven't been surrounded by really beautiful girls for your entire life, that my initial reaction—"

Glin put his hand over her mouth. "I like you. You like me. Is this right? Don't speak."

Luci nodded.

"Fine. That's settled. Let's go back."

Chapter Four

Dinner was served in the formal dining room, a huge space that could easily seat twenty-four guests. There were portraits of the previous owners on the wall as well as sabers, antique rifles, and tapestries. They heard stories of the grand people who had stayed at the lodge over the years: George Bernard Shaw, Winston Churchill, William Butler Yeats, and Daniel O'Connell, the Irish statesman.

Tess went from one guest to another under the table, nudging their feet for a handout and looking pathetic.

Stacey looked down. "What does this dog want from me?"

Siobhan smiled. "She hasn't learned her table manners."

Luci imagined the dog sitting in a chair, knowing which fork to use for her salad and which was the soup spoon. She laughed to herself. Tess didn't seem a promising candidate for a course in etiquette—she was too hungry.

Tess grabbed onto the bottom of Stacey's trousers and began to pull.

"Will you let go?" Stacey commanded as she tried to wrench her leg away. "These are Ralph Lauren trousers!"

Tess was unimpressed and began to growl playfully.

Siobhan stood and scooped Tess into her arms. "Sorry. I'll lock her in the pantry."

As the dinner plates were being cleared, Daria spoke up. "Fran said something about a foxhunt in the area."

Liam leaned back. "The Blazers. I've belonged to the group for years. A fine group of people."

"Very energetic," Siobhan added.

"That we are. Hunting is a way of life for most of us and we meet several times a week. I'm going tomorrow, if anyone's interested."

"I am," Daria replied quickly.

"Me, too," Logan agreed.

"Do you have any experience?" Siobhan asked.

"I've hunted in California," Daria replied.

Stacey folded her napkin carefully. "So have I."

"I've hunted on horseback," Logan said. "Not foxhunting. We were after bigger game."

"What would that be? Pterodactyls?" Jay asked.

"Elk," Logan replied.

"Water buffalo?" Jay continued.

Logan shook his head.

Siobhan returned to the dining room without

Tess. "We've combed Ireland and England for used hunting outfits, so we have something to fit everyone. If you all want to go, I'm sure we have clothes."

"I don't ride well enough for that," Luci demurred.

"I'm in that camp," Jay agreed.

"Not to worry," Siobhan interjected. "There are a group of novice riders, as well as older riders or younger riders who don't feel comfortable keeping up with the pack. They ride off to the side and are called hill-toppers. The fastest they ever go is a trot."

Luci and Jay exchanged doubtful glances.

"The funny thing about the hill-toppers is that most of the time they get to the fox before the hounds or the rest of the hunt. I don't know how that happens," Siobhan declared.

Fran grew enthusiastic. "It's a rare experience to be able to ride with a traditional Irish hunt."

Luci looked at her. "Are you going?"

"I'd love to."

"Do you know how to ride?" Jay asked.

"I can get by," Fran replied.

Siobhan laughed. "Don't let her modesty fool you. Fran's an excellent rider."

Luci glanced around the table. They all rode. "Aimee, do you ride?"

Aimee smiled. "I imagine I could stay on. I've had several past lives where I rode extensively."

Jay kicked at Luci's foot under the table. Luci knew what that meant. Why do you ask her?

"I'll go with the hill-topper group, and if you want to stop at any point, we can go home," Siobhan offered.

Luci knew they weren't going to get out of this. A feeling of dread began to overtake her. She could imagine how much trouble she could get into riding with a group of people far more expert than she. What if the horse decided he wanted to run and she didn't want him to? What if she lost her stirrups? Or dropped her reins? Or needed to blow her nose at the wrong moment? What if they came upon the fox and it scared her horse?

What if she fell off in front of everyone?

"What time do you meet?" Stacey asked.

"Six A.M.," Siobhan answered.

"You mean you get up at six," Jay said.

"No. We're mounted and the horn's blowing at six. We get up at four."

"Terrific!" Logan exclaimed.

Luci sighed. Someone had broken their promise to her! It was supposed to be pony trekking. It was supposed to be walking down quiet Irish lanes admiring the quaint villages. It was supposed to be a vacation!

"We haven't slept in thirty-six hours," Jay commented when they got to their room. "And now we're getting up at four to go plunging through the underbrush?" She didn't have any more confidence in her riding ability than Luci had in her own. Jay was seriously doubting the wisdom of this decision already, believing far greater equestrian experience was required of those expecting to keep up with a hunt. She had seen films of hunts. It seemed like madness to her.

Luci put down all the clothes Siobhan had given her—a white shirt, breeches, boots, a black hunt coat. She picked up the bowler Siobhan had given her and grimaced. "I'm supposed to wear this pot on my head? I'll look ridiculous."

"No more than me!" Jay shoved the hat on her own head, her hair sticking out from under it in all directions. She held up a fistful of hair. "How am I supposed to get all this into this?" She held up a tiny hair net.

"Maybe you could put it into a bun and tie a scarf around it," Luci suggested.

Jay wrestled with her hair. "I'll have to get up at three, just to do this!"

"Let's just promise not to leave each other's side."

"Good idea." Jay flopped onto the bed.

Luci flipped on the television.

"What's on?"

On the screen were four people sitting at a long table. Luci and Jay listened for a minute in confusion.

"They're talking about roundabouts," Luci said.

"Those circular things in the road?" Jay asked.

Roundabouts were often used in place of traffic lights out in the country where four roads intersected. They kept the traffic moving without causing confusion as to which vehicle should move next.

"Yeah." Luci couldn't believe it either.

"Next!"

Luci turned the dial and stopped at the only other channel. Krystle Carrington. *Dynasty*. Bleech."

Luci turned off the television. "We've got an early morning anyway."

"You're right."

Luci finished unpacking.

"Did you have a chance to work things out with Glin?" Jay asked her.

"He worked things out with me, I guess."

"Good. I don't have to worry about that anymore."

There was a scream.

Luci was dreaming. Logan was leaning too far over the Cliffs of Moher and went off the edge. Luci saw him falling, falling, down, farther and farther to the rocks below. There was a scream. Suddenly Logan began to fly. He had sprouted wings and was flying up into the sky.

"Luci! Wake up!"

"What?"

"Wake up!"

There was another scream.

This one wasn't part of a dream and Jay was standing next to her bed.

"What's wrong?" Luci asked, trying to wake up.

There was yet another scream.

"Did you hear that?"

"Yes! Is the door locked?"

"Put on your robe and let's go find out who it is!"

Jay pushed Luci's robe in her face and raced for the door.

Luci dragged herself out of bed and pulled on the robe. She wasn't sure she wanted to find out who had screamed. It sounded terrible, like something she didn't want to be involved in.

Jay had already disappeared down the hall by the time Luci reached the door. She could hear voices now. The activity seemed to be coming from the upstairs hallway.

The hallway seemed endless as Luci made her way through the turns and twists until she finally reached the foyer. The voices were louder and she ran up the front stairs, pulling her robe tighter around her.

"I'm telling you the truth!" Stacey insisted.

"Calm down," Fran said.

"I know when it's time to calm down and this isn't the time for it!" Stacey couldn't have been speaking any faster.

"Is there a fire?" Jay asked.

"It's no fire," Logan replied in disgust.

Daria was shrinking back against the wall.

Aimee came out of her room, no robe, no shoes, just a huge T-shirt hanging down halfway to her knees. "Am I missing something?"

"I was attacked!" Stacey screamed.

"Attacked?" Luci nearly fell over.

Glin put his hand on her arm. "She's exaggerating."

"I am not! You weren't there. I was. I was attacked!"

"By who?" Fran asked.

"I couldn't see. The room was dark."

Fran and Siobhan exchanged worried glances. "Stacey, please, try to tell us what happened."

"Someone came in the room!"

Liam frowned. "All the doors are locked, and we have an alarm system. There was no one in the house but us. We have day help, but they don't live on the property."

"I couldn't see who it was."

"If it wasn't a stranger . . ." Daria began.

"It was one of us," Glin replied.

Logan shook his head. "Was your door locked?"

"Of course!"

"So what happened? The guy came in the window? We're three floors up!" Logan pointed out.

"Hang on," Fran said. "Let's not assume the worst. We still haven't heard what happened. Stacey, can you tell us?"

"I was awakened by someone pressing on my bed."

"Huh?" Logan grunted.

Stacey made a pressing motion with both hands. "Down at the footboard. I could feel the bed rocking."

Jay shook her head. "You were dreaming."

"Thank you very much. I was not dreaming."

"How do you know?" Jay retorted.

"Because when I woke up and felt the bed moving, I asked myself if I was dreaming. And I said no."

Logan turned away.

Fran put her hand on Stacey's shoulder. "Dreams can be very vivid."

"Maybe you were dreaming you were awake," Luci offered.

"Maybe you were dreaming you were asleep and dreamed you were awake dreaming you were being attacked. . . ." Logan added.

"Will you please listen to me!" Stacey shouted. "I was asleep. The bed started moving. It woke me up."

"Are you sure you weren't moving the bed?" Glin asked.

"I was so scared I was paralyzed. I felt each arm and leg and none of them were moving!" Stacey whirled. "If it was anyone else, you'd believe them!"

Fran took a hold of Stacey's arm. "That's not true. We're just trying to find out what happened."

Stacey grimaced. "I told you! I was attacked!"

"Then where's the culprit?" Glin asked.

"If there was someone in your room, they either left your room when you screamed or they're still in there," Logan said as he marched down the hall to Stacey's room.

He flung open the door and flipped on the light. A moment later he returned to the hallway. "There's no one in there. The window's locked."

"Did you see or hear the door open?" Liam asked.

"No."

Aimee smiled. "It's a ghost."

Daria turned pale.

Luci caught her breath.

"Aimee, please," Fran said.

"It's very common for an entity to move a bed in order to get attention."

"You're not helping," Fran said quietly.

"Keep talking, Aimee," Stacey interjected.

"A spirit who feels ignored often has a temper tantrum."

"There are no such things as ghosts," Logan replied.

Aimee turned to him. "How do you know that?"

"Because a rational person requires physical proof of these harebrained allegations. There is no Loch Ness Monster. There are no ghosts. And no tooth fairy!"

Aimee shrugged. "That's fine. I'm sure this ghost doesn't care if you believe in him or not."

Fran sighed. "There are no ghosts."

Siobhan shifted her weight from one foot to the other. "Actually, it's said that a ghost does roam this house."

Fran glared at Siobhan.

"I'm not saying I believe it. We bought the house and the previous owners warned us . . ."

"Siobhan . . ." Liam began.

"Very well. Warn is too strong a word. They told us rocking chairs would rock . . ."

"Someone was walking on the floor and the vibration caused the chair to move," Logan replied.

". . . and doors would bang . . ." Siobhan continued.

"Wind," Logan commented.

"They would find windows open that they had locked."

"Amnesia," Logan persisted.

"I'm just telling you what they said."

"Don't." Daria's voice shook.

"Why don't we all try to get back to sleep. We do have an early morning," Liam suggested.

"I don't want to go back in that room," Daria insisted.

"Nice going, Aimee," Fran said in resignation.

"We'll stay in the room, and they can have ours," Logan offered.

Glin nodded. "Sure. No problem."

Daria smiled gratefully. "Thank you."

"They've slept on those sheets," Stacey protested.

Logan leaned toward her. "We both took a shower!"

Jay grinned at Luci. "She's doing it again!"

Luci began laughing. In France, Stacey refused to use the same toilet as the rest of the group unless she put down several layers of paper.

Stacey glared at her and Luci bit her lip, trying to behave herself.

Fran raised her hands. "It's up to you. The boys have very generously offered their room. If you don't want to take it, we won't force the issue."

Stacey stomped down the hallway. "I don't really have any choice, do I?" she disappeared into her room. "Daria's going to cut and run. What am I going to do?" She appeared, her arms full of her night things. "Room with the Exorcist there?" She motioned toward Aimee.

Fran turned to Aimee. "She doesn't mean that. She's just upset."

"That's okay," Aimee replied. "I don't mind."

Daria dashed down the hall to scoot into the new room before Stacey slammed the door.

"I guess the fun's over for the night." Fran grinned.

Jay groaned. "It's not worth it to go back to sleep."

"Okay, Glin," Fran said. "Back to your room."

Glin smiled at Luci. "See you tomorrow."

"Today," Luci corrected, and went down the stairs. A moment later she heard the door to Glin's room close.

Chapter Five

Luci couldn't believe she was on a horse at six A.M. They hadn't even had breakfast. That was supposed to come after all this dashing around. All she had been able to grab was a piece of bread, an apple, and a wedge of Blarney cheese, which she shared with Jay as they helped each other dress.

All that dressing had to get easier with practice or someone needed to invent a way to put zippers and snaps where there weren't any. The tall boots were the most difficult. She and Jay had hopped around the room trying to jam their legs into the leather stovepipes.

"What are we supposed to be singing?" Jay had growled as she flipped her hair back over her shoulder. "A-hunting we will go, a hunting we will go, high-ho the derry-o . . ."

"Please don't," Luci huffed as she finally found the bottom of the boot. "Let's make this a positive experience."

"*Ha!*"

Now they were all gathered on the main street of Ballynahinch. A fine mist was falling, fog moved and swirled, and it was cool enough to require gloves.

Luci and Jay huddled together by the horse trailer.

"How long is this going to take?" Luci wondered.

"Three or four hours?"

"I thought it was going to be an hour, tops."

The town square was now full of horses, riders and hounds. People greeted each other, laughing, unconcerned about the weather.

Logan rode by on Balar, who was bucking and twisting.

Jay thought she saw a spark fly up from a horseshoe as it struck the pavement. "I don't think so."

"Do you think there was a ghost in Stacey's room?"

"No."

"What do you think it was?"

"She was dreaming."

Luci wasn't willing to believe it was a ghost, but she also didn't think Stacey was prone to hallucinations.

Aimee rode up, appearing completely comfortable on her horse. "The hunt breakfast will be at the Humanity Dick."

"Excuse me?" Luci said.

Aimee pointed to the public house across the street. An old sign hung on the front reading HUMANITY DICK.

"What does that mean?" Jay asked.

Aimee shrugged.

Just then, several cars pulled up in front of the pub and about a dozen people got out, dragging signs out of the trunks, or boots as they were called in Ireland.

"The picketers!" Jay exclaimed.

Sure enough, it was. They lined themselves upon the sidewalk and held up their signs, proudly protesting the hunt.

"I don't feel good about this," Luci said.

"It would be better if someone wasn't here—us or them."

"They have the right to their beliefs," Aimee commented.

"But doesn't it seem a little odd for all of us on big strong horses, with dogs with big sharp teeth to go chasing after a little fox?" Luci said.

"Lots of things people do are odd."

"But does it seem right?" Jay asked.

"What seems right to some would be wrong to others."

Aimee was going to be no help at all.

The picketers silently stood and glared at the riders.

"Some vacation!" Stacey snapped as she rode up. "I travel six thousand miles to be reviled!" She was wearing her own riding clothes, which were impeccable. A black jacket nipped in at the waist, white skintight breeches, black Spanish top boots. Her auburn hair was in a net, perfectly flipped under, not a strand out of place.

"Did you tie your own . . ." Jay pointed at her neck.

"Of course!" Stacey replied.

Jay and Luci had stood patiently while Siobhan had tied their stocks for them, after they had tossed the long ends of the stock tie back and forth many times, only to wind up with big knots at their necks instead of the graceful folds Stacey was sporting. Topped by the traditional gold stock pin. Jay and Luci had blanket pins.

Jay studied Stacey's tie. "Couldn't they invent a pretied thing you could just loop around your neck and go?"

Stacey regarded Jay as though she were hopeless. "What if you're out in the field and you get hurt? This is a bandage. The pin will keep it on until you get to a doctor. You can't fake this."

Jay leaned over and whispered, "This doesn't sound good."

"Don't think about it," Luci whispered back. "Stacey, who are all those people?" She pointed to the riders.

Stacey glanced across the town square. "Everyone wearing red is a staff member. Only they are allowed to wear red."

"Their hats are different," Jay noted.

"Men wear hunt caps. Staff members, male or female, wear hunt caps. Ladies wear bowlers. Children wear hunt caps."

"What's the good of wearing this bowler if it has to be tied to my coat?" Jay asked, flipping the cord attached to her jacket.

"It's for tradition, not protection."

Jay grimaced. "Brilliant. No wonder they need bandages."

All this was more than Luci had ever wanted to know about hunt chapeau protocol.

"Only male members of the hunt wear boots with tan tops. Women staff members may wear patent-leather tops. Everyone else wears plain black. During cubbing season you may wear field boots, since it's less formal," Stacey explained.

"You must have done a lot of this," Jay said.

"When my father worked in New York, we hunted with the Rombout Hunt Club."

Luci was surprised. "Then your father rides, too."

"Yes. Is that unusual?"

Luci laughed. "My father certainly doesn't ride."

Jay grinned. "The only thing my father would have ridden would be his ship if it was coming in."

"That's the master of foxhounds, whose word is law. Those are huntsmen. Those are whips," Stacey explained.

Jay glanced at the riders. "Whips, huh?"

"They keep keep the hounds in line."

Daria trotted up. "This is great." Her horse snorted large puffs of steam from both nostrils.

Luci's horse was asleep, and for that she was grateful.

"What's their problem?" Daria asked, motioning toward the protesters.

"To them we're disgusting animal abusers," Jay replied.

"I'm not an animal abuser. I've never hurt an animal in my life!" Luci protested.

"Tell that to the woman coming over here to yell at us," Jay remarked.

Sure enough, there was an older woman striding across the town square, headed directly toward them.

"See you guys later," Daria called as she trotted away.

"Coward!" Stacey called back.

The tall, gray-haired woman stopped by the girls. "Good morning, ladies. I'm Ethne Coughlin."

"Good morning."

"You must be Americans."

They nodded.

"We would be so much happier if you didn't support this hunt."

"We're only here for a couple of days," Stacey explained.

"Yes, but your presence encourages the tormenting of helpless animals. We want to put an end to this abuse."

Siobhan approached. "Good morning, Ethne."

"Siobhan." The older woman nodded.

"Come along, girls, it's time to begin."

Siobhan herded them closer to the square, where the other riders were gathering.

Fran joined them. "Okay, guys, listen to me. We are the newcomers, so we stay behind. Stacey, you're going in with the field, aren't you?"

"Yes."

"Okay. See you later. Mind your etiquette."

"Of course," Stacey replied, moving toward Liam, Logan, Daria, and Glin. Princess Anne couldn't have been more regal.

"If you feel uncomfortable," Fran continued, "let me know and we can turn around. Aimee, please take the earphones off." Fran motioned toward Aimee's ears.

Aimee removed her bowler, then the earphones, and replaced the bowler. It looked like a black cauldron on her head.

"We'll probably be out here two or three hours," Siobhan went on. "It should be an easy ride."

"Two or three hours?" Luci gasped. She'd never been on a horse for more than an hour. The length of one lesson.

The huntsman blew a horn.

"Hark to the horn!" someone shouted.

The foxhounds yelped, wailed, and barked as the field began to walk down the street.

Despite herself, Luci felt a wave of excitement wash over her. It was like being in an old English print. It was like being with Jackie Kennedy Onassis and her high-society friends.

She glanced toward the protesters.

It was like being a criminal!

From the top of the hill, they could see the field racing below them. The tan-and-white English foxhounds were far in the lead, followed by riders in red coats, followed by the field. Luci strained to see Glin but couldn't pick him out from the distance.

"There's Logan!" Jay pointed.

"How can you tell?"

"The blond hair and that's the only horse plunging across the field."

Luci nodded. Jay was correct. That was Logan, right behind the members of the hunt. The horse seemed to be struggling to get ahead of the rest of the riders.

Fran sighed. "Maybe Logan will be tired tonight."

Luci raised an eyebrow.

"Or not," Fran admitted.

The barking of the hounds sounded thin through the fog and in a moment they disappeared over a stone wall and down a hill. The hill-toppers moved off along the ridge, parallel to the hunt at a slow trot.

Luci was feeling fairly secure. Her horse seemed to be very gentle and by all indications would have preferred to be back in the barn munching on some hay.

Down in the valley, Glin and Logan were racing along with the rest of the hunt. Luci began to entertain notions of renting a horse and riding through Central Park so she could become a more proficient rider.

Jay came up beside her as they continued along the hill. "This is not anything for me. I'm cold, I'm wet, and the insides of my knees are raw."

Luci was feeling it in another part of her anatomy.

"Why can't we wear raincoats?" Jay asked.

The horses picked their way down the rocky hillside.

"It's not permitted," Siobhan said over her shoulder.

"Does that make any sense to you?" Jay asked Luci.

"No."

"It's raining."

"It's soft," Siobhan replied.

Fran reined in her horse. "That's an Irish term for a day like this."

"The soft is someplace else. Like in the head," Jay whispered. "No one should be out on a day like this."

"Most of the days are like this," Fran replied.

Aimee smiled. "It's quite beautiful. You can feel the vibrations. . . ."

"Yeah," Jay said shortly. She had had enough of the otherworld last night.

"What's going on over there?" Aimee asked.

The hill-toppers stopped to see where she was pointing.

There was a group of people throwing rocks from a stone wall into what was obviously the path of the riders.

"It's that woman!" Luci said.

"Ethne," Siobhan supplied. "She's always been the local character, but in the last couple years I must say she's outdone herself."

They resumed their trek toward the people on foot.

The barking of the hounds grew louder. Soon horses appeared. The protesters stood their ground.

"Get out of the way!" the master shouted.

"You'll have to go over me," Ethne shouted back.

"Ethne! Go home!"

"I will not. What you're doing is wrong and it must be stopped."

Siobhan halted her horse near Luci, Jay, and Fran. "That's Brendan O'Rahilly." She pointed at the master. "He and Ethne were an item thirty years ago."

"What happened?" Jay asked, fascinated.

"No one knows. It seemed, I'm told, they were going to get married. And then they didn't. People say they haven't spoken since."

"Until today?" Luci asked in amazement.

"It may well be."

"They're probably soul mates. It's so hard to keep two people apart who were meant to be together," Aimee commented.

"What if they're meant to be enemies?" Jay asked.

"If they were going to get married, they weren't enemies. Not at the soul level."

Luci shrugged at Jay.

Ethne and Brendan had faced off, but other staff members were picking their way over the wall farther down the field. Logan flashed by, his horse's nostrils flared and red.

Luci searched the field for Glin and finally placed him halfway back just as his horse jumped the wall and made a sharp turn to the right.

Fran crossed her hands in front of her over the pommel of her saddle. "What say we go back?"

"You've got my vote," Luci replied quickly, and they all turned their horses around.

The pub was quiet, since only the hill-toppers had arrived. The group had returned to the town square, taken care of their horses, put them in the horse trailer with hay, and then walked across the street to Humanity Dick. They found seats along the window and made themselves comfortable.

"Humanity Dick lived here many years ago. He was a member of Parliament and was active in the Royal Society for the Prevention of Cruelty to Animals," Siobhan explained.

"Ironic," Aimee said.

They waited for her to say more, but that was it.

"The hunt meets in a pub named after a man who would have been furious that they hunt foxes," Luci was struggling to follow the logic.

"I don't think I want to go hunting again," Jay remarked.

"I wish Ethne hadn't spoiled it for you," Siobhan said.

"I'm glad to know the other side of the story. Boy, I'm glad we didn't *see* anything," Luci replied.

"It's very unusual for the hounds to catch up with the fox," Siobhan assured them.

"But it does happen," Jay said.

"Of course. Foxes can be a real problem to farmers. They are predators."

Luci took a sip of tea. "You all may be cut out for that, but I'm not."

Siobhan looked over her shoulder. "The field's back."

There was a clatter of hooves on the pavement as the field came back to the town square.

"I don't think they had a very good day. Liam won't be pleased," Siobhan said.

Luci leaned over to Fran. "Let's go someplace this afternoon that won't cause an argument."

"Good suggestion," Fran agreed.

"It was wonderful. You should have been there!" Logan scooped a spoonful of steak and kidney pie from the buffet onto his plate.

"We *were* there," Jay reminded him.

"Not with the field."

"Thank goodness," Luci replied.

"We went down a hill that was so steep, my horse was on his tail. At the bottom was a four-foot fence. Right over it!" Logan motioned up and down with his hand.

Luci's stomach twisted just imagining it.

"How was your ride?" Glin asked as he followed her along in the line.

"I'm glad we did it. Once."

"It wasn't a very nice day. If it had been dry and clear, maybe you would have enjoyed it more."

The door was flung open. "Brendan!" Ethne cried out.

Everyone went silent. Forks stopped in midair on the way to mouths. Plates hovered above steaming trays of food. Tea ceased to be poured.

Master O'Rahilly turned. He was a large man. Imposing, with a full head of gray hair.

"You must stop this madness!" Ethne continued.

He said nothing. In three strides, he reached Ethne, grabbed her by the arm, and pushed her unceremoniously out the door. He shut the door behind her and twisted the lock.

A moment later she was rapping at the window. Calling out, protesting.

"Let the breakfast continue," Brendan O'Rahilly said evenly as he went back to his staff.

Chapter Six

"**W**hat a day. First we have ghosts and then we have animal-rights protesters," Luci remarked later as she peeled off her damp breeches.

Jay was hopping around the room, trying to remove her boot. "And we've only been here twenty-four hours. What else can happen to us?"

"Maybe it's better if we don't ask. We may draw it to us."

"Stop talking to Aimee!" Jay exclaimed as the boot finally came free and she sprawled on the floor in exhaustion.

Luci pulled her soft, dry terrycloth robe around her and it felt so good. "Wasn't this a case of misrepresentation? We were supposed to go pony trekking!"

"Cute little ponies and picnic baskets!" Jay agreed.

Luci folded the breeches and put them to the side. "We really do have to protest this, don't we?"

"I'd say so."

"Do you want to shower first?"

"No. You go. I want to recuperate."

Luci picked up her shower things and went into the bathroom. She had envisioned this trip quite differently than it was turning out. As she stepped into the tub the hot water poured over her. Maybe she had been fantasizing. Maybe she hadn't been realistic. She'd had the image of them walking down old Irish streets, laughing at donkeys standing in the doorways of blue farm cottages, and gazing in awe at stunning scenery.

It was all in the travel brochures!

There had been no donkeys so far, she had been more worried about steering her horse than appreciating the street, and the scenery had been lost in the fog.

And Glin.

Well, she didn't really know what she had expected there. A couple of moments of being alone?

Last night, after the ghost scare, she really thought Glin was going to walk her back to the room, but Fran had gotten in the way of that.

Luci closed her eyes and stood under the stream of water.

Jay rapped on the door.

"What?"

"Can I come in?"

"Is it an emergency? Yeah. Yeah."

"I won't look."

"Well, thank you for that."

Jay entered with her eyes averted. "Listen, we have to do something about this trip or it's going to go down the . . ." She pointed to the porcelain facility.

"I agree, but what?"

"We have to get away from this place."

"We're booked to stay here!"

"So we do day trips! We come back after all chance of being involved with the Connemara Blazers is shot."

"All right."

"I'm going to go look up all the attractions within a four-hour drive and we're going to insist we do all of them. As long as we're not here, we can't do the trekking stuff."

"What about Stacey, Daria, and Logan? They're here to ride."

"We'll outvote them."

"If Aimee votes with us."

"Aimee will agree with whoever gets to her first," Jay pointed out reasonably.

Luci nodded. That was true. "Go get her."

Jay was out of the bathroom before she could reply.

Luci was drying her hair when Jay came back with Aimee.

"We have a proposal," Jay began.

Aimee smiled.

"We don't want to go hunting anymore."

"Why not?"

"Because I don't want to cross a picket line."

Luci glanced at Jay. "Is that true?"

"Close enough."

Aimee shrugged. "There will always be conflicting opinions in the world. This is a plane of duality. Either/or. Night/day. Black/white. Male/female. This is the natural order of things."

"I don't care about the duality," Jay replied.

"But you do," Aimee insisted. "You've taken a position. You think that hunting is wrong. Now there are two sides. You created the conflict in your mind."

Jay looked to Luci in despair. This is getting into a realm neither wanted to traverse.

"Do you have a side in this?" Luci asked.

Aimee shook her head. "No."

"Then do you mind if we do something else? We've done the hunting. Now . . . can we have some other experiences?"

"We're here to experience. Only by going through the process can we grow and learn. That's enlightenment."

"Does that mean you'll go along with us?" Jay asked.

Aimee nodded. "Sure."

Two hours later they were all in the van travelling on the road to Kylemore Abbey through the Lough Inagh Valley. Luci was satisfied. The scenery was fantastic now that the fog had lifted, and she could see green hills stretching to the mountains.

"Liam says we can go hunting again this week, and just before we leave, there's going to be a blessing of the hounds," Logan offered.

Jay threw Luci a look.

Luci felt the panic, too. But she didn't know what

to do other than splitting the group up. Actually, as she thought about it, that seemed the most sensible solution. If Fran would go along with it.

"There are other things to do," Glin said.

"Like?"

"Like visiting Kylemore Abbey," Fran replied as she turned into the driveway. "It was built for Mitchell Henry. He was yet another Englishman who fell in love with Ireland when he spent his honeymoon in Connemara. Years later a group of Benedictine nuns left Belgium and found a home here. There's a convent school and a tearoom." Fran stopped the van.

They stopped to stare at the gray, towering, castlelike structure and the beautiful placid lake in front of it.

They went to the front door. It was locked.

Fran tried again. She couldn't budge it.

"Fran . . ." Luci began.

"Not to worry," Fran told them, and knocked sharply on the huge wooden door.

Several minutes passed, then they heard the bolt slide and the door opened a few inches.

"May I help you?" a nun asked.

"We're here for the tour."

"I'm sorry, we're closed."

Luci could hear Stacey snort in disgust.

Jay grabbed Luci's arm and hissed in her ear, "This doesn't look good for us!"

"You may walk around the gardens if you wish," the nun offered, and the door was closed.

Logan nodded. "That was really great." He burst

into laughter. Glin began smiling and soon was doubled over, too.

Fran turned. "Okay, ladies and gentlemen. This is not a perfect world."

"If it were perfect, we wouldn't need to be here," Aimee offered.

Fran regarded Aimee for a long moment. "Yes. Right. Kylemore Abbey is lovely and you would have enjoyed it. We can go on to Clifden. That's quite an interesting town. Many things to see."

The group moved back to the van. Jay stopped Luci.

"There's nothing to see in Clifden."

"How do you know?"

"I read the book."

"Girls," Fran called from the van. "Let's move out."

Jay looked at Luci. "Fifteen minutes, tops, in Clifden."

Fran found a parking place easily along the near-deserted main street of Clifden.

"I'm hungry," Daria said.

Fran turned to the others. "We'll find a restaurant. Do we want to eat here?"

"Yes!" Jay replied quickly.

"I'd rather go back," Stacey countered.

"We'll be at River House for three meals a day all week . . ." Logan began.

Luci and Jay shared a look.

"Let's try someplace else tonight," Logan finished.

"There must be a club or something," Glin suggested.

"Good idea. I'm sure there is," Fran agreed. "Didn't you like the waterfalls on the River Owenglin?"

No one replied.

Fran stopped on the street. "What is with you kids? Is it me? Am I not doing something?"

"No one's complaining," Jay said. Not exactly.

"It's jet lag," Glin suggested.

"Maybe it's hunger pangs," Luci offered.

Logan glanced up the street. "There's a restaurant. It'll solve all the problems." He ran up the sidewalk and just as quickly came back.

Jay shook her head. "What?"

"It doesn't open until seven."

Daria wailed.

"This is Europe," Fran replied. "They eat late."

"Is there a McDonald's in town?" Stacey asked.

"No McDonald's!" Luci nearly shouted.

Everyone stared at her.

Luci blushed. "What I meant to say is that we all know exactly what you can get at McDonald's. And that uniformity is a wonderful thing. But while we're here, shouldn't we try to experience Irish culture?"

Glin applauded.

"But I'm hungry now!"

"Go get a candy bar," Fran said. "There's a newsstand right there. We'll wait for you. Anyone else who needs something, go get it now."

Daria went up the street.

"Any suggestions?" Fran asked.

"You've been here before, we haven't," Luci said. "I'm perfectly happy with everything right now. Aren't you, Jay?"

"Perfectly. And it's only two hours till dinner, so I can wait for that."

Logan looked at them. "What's going on?"

"Nothing," Luci replied quickly. "I think Glin was probably right. Jet lag and ghosts. We're all tired."

Please, someone believe that.

"That's right," Stacey agreed.

Luci couldn't believe she was hearing correctly. Stacey agreed with her? She must be very tired.

Logan was disgusted. "Take some vitamins."

Daria returned with assorted candy bars and treats.

"Back in the van," Fran said. "This one's for Logan."

Several minutes later Fran stopped the van on the way to Ballyconneely. "Here we are."

"Another ruin. Gee, what a surprise," Stacey commented as they all got out of the vehicle.

"That is not just another ruin," Fran insisted. "That is a wireless station built in 1906 by Guglielmo Marconi for his first transatlantic communications."

Stacey nodded but appeared less than impressed.

"Careful going here, this is a bog," Fran said as they crossed through a pasture. "Derrygimlagh Bog to be precise."

The ground squished as they walked to a small memorial.

Fran looked at Logan. "Why is this significant?"

Logan beamed. "Back in 1919, even though airplanes had been used extensively in World War One, they had been flown short-range and over-ground. It was thought that a nonstop transatlantic flight was impossible. It had been tried, and quite a few pilots had died. Don't forget we're talking about aircraft made of wood and canvas. They had small engines and not great lifting capacity. But two men, John Alcock and Arthur Brown, thought they could make the flight. They left St. John's, Newfoundland, in their Vicker Vimy and of course everyone assumed they would be lost. On June fifteenth, 1919, they wound up here. Not exactly a three-point landing, unless you call falling on your nose one of the points. But it was the first successful transatlantic flight."

"I thought Lindbergh was the first and it was much later," Stacey said.

"Charles Lindbergh flew farther. He went from New York to Paris and he did it alone in 1927."

"With the attention of the entire world," Luci said.

"It was a different world ten years later," Glin agreed.

"These guys were real heroes and my shoes are getting wet," Stacey replied.

"Time to go back to town." Fran shrugged.

Mannin's Pub was chosen among the various hotels and cafés on Clifden's main street because of the large sign outside advertising the Roundstone Band, which played traditional music.

Dinner was traditional—boiled beef and cabbage, Irish stew, or plaice, a fish none of them were familiar with. Dessert was a double-crust apple pie served with custard.

As they finished the meal the band mounted the stage to cheers and applause. They immediately began singing a song in Irish that none of the tourists recognized. There was more applause as the leader stood up to the microphone.

"A very good evening to you. We're the Roundstone Band. I'm Dennis. That's Ciaran, Seamus, Declan, and James. This is a traditional song called 'Bhean a Ti,' which means old woman of the house, what ails you?"

One after another the songs continued, some slow, some fast, some sad, some joyous. By the time "Dheanainn Sugradh" was being played, the audience was on their feet dancing. "Nil Se'n La" had everyone clapping and singing along.

The applause was fierce as the band left the small stage.

"They were fantastic!" Jay enthused.

Fran smiled. "So the evening is a hit."

"Yes!" everyone said in unison.

"Finally." Fran sighed and wiped her forehead. "I thought I was losing my touch!"

"Never," Logan assured her.

Luci noticed the empty seat next to her. "Where's Glin?"

"By all appearances, it was a perfect evening and now one of you is lost," Fran groaned.

"He'll turn up."

"I'll have a look around," Luci offered as she pushed back from the table.

"Buddy system!" Fran called out.

Jay stood and followed Luci toward the rest rooms.

"What are you going to do? Bang on the door? What if it's full of Irishmen?"

"And it would look silly to stand there." Luci continued down the narrow hall. "So we won't do that."

They heard laughter and followed the sound of the voices. Turning a corner, they came upon the tiny dressing room. The band was inside and so was Glin. He looked up as the girls came to the doorway.

"Come on in!" He motioned to them.

Musical instruments were everywhere. There were boxes, trunks, and metal cases. A plate of half-eaten sandwiches rested on a table lamp while wires snaked on the floor. Luci and Jay squeezed into the tight space as they were introduced to the group.

Names, musical terms, and song titles were tossed back and forth so quickly there was no hope for Luci to keep up with the conversation.

"And Finn Lunny, you've heard of him," Glin said.

"Who hasn't?"

"Finn's a master of the uileann pipes," Seamus admitted.

"The lad can play anything," Dennis replied.

"A private sort. We used to see him around. One or two years ago? I can't say I've heard anything of him since."

Glin persisted. "He's from the west coast."

"That he is. North of here."

"But he was living in Westport."

"Yes, yes. We played a gig at Oisin's and someone told us they had seen him at the Dulaman. Wasn't that it?"

The members of the band agreed.

"How far is Westport from here?" Glin asked.

"Two hours or so. It's on the ocean."

"We're on the ocean." Someone laughed.

"So we are! But it's further west. Are you going to look Lunny up?"

"It would be nice," Glin replied.

"Then you give him our regards and tell him he can play with us anytime he wants."

"Which will be the twelfth of never!" someone joked.

"I can only dream of being as good as Lunny." Dennis sighed. "Good luck on tracking him down; you'll need it."

Glin shook everyone's hand and they left the dressing room.

"So you want to go off to find this man?" Luci asked.

"It would be nice."

Luci and Jay exchanged a glance.

"Only it wouldn't be fair to everyone else," Glin replied.

"Sure it would be!"

Luci nodded. "I'm all for it."

Chapter Seven

There was a fire in the sizable brick fireplace. Liam had thrown several logs on the blaze earlier in the evening and they were still burning brightly when the grandfather clock chimed eleven.

Luci felt tired but not sleepy. Besides, it was too pleasant sitting in this comfortable room with her friends to entertain notions of going back to the room. She sipped at her hot chocolate, which was now barely lukewarm, nibbled on a biscuit, and sank deeper into the cushions of the sofa.

Everything about the room made her feel like staying longer. The walls were covered with a pale cream-colored linen wallpaper. Heavy drapes were drawn in front of the large windows. There were many oil paintings; several were landscapes, one was a still life with brilliant red peonies in a vase, another was a hunting scene. Antique furniture was dark and burnished to a high sheen. The dark red Oriental carpet was old and quite worn in some areas.

Siobhan and Liam had obviously thought very carefully about how to make this house as attractive for guests as possible, and they had succeeded. It felt like a home rather than a hotel.

Luci wondered what it would be like to live in such a spacious house. There was certainly storage capacity for several families. In the McKennitts' apartment in the city, space was at a premium. Clothes that weren't worn were donated to charity, not pushed to the rear of the closet and forgotten. There was no room for clutter or collections. All that had taught Luci how to make use of every square inch she had.

But this was a house where people could move around without bumping into each other. There was a terrific attic that could contain generations of old clothes. There were so many rooms that they were named to distinguish between them.

For example, there was the library where people could gather, but there was also the blue room—a large living room being decorated in various shades of blue. Not quite ready for company yet, it would be spectacular when completed.

The house was so big, it was conceivable that a guest could get lost once or twice before he got his bearings. But still there was a coziness about the library, with the porcelain table lamps casting a soft yellow glow and the fire dancing in the hearth.

Outside was the river and the dark night.

Inside were tales of old Ireland. "The first residents of Ireland were the Fir Bolg. At that time, before the written word, the Tuatha De Danann lived on the northern islands. They were the people of the goddess Danu and they had four great cities. In each of these cities was a wizard whose magical skills and knowledge surpassed that of any people before or since. There was Morfesa, Esras, Semias, and Uiscias.

"However, the Tuatha De wanted a new homeland. A green land, fertile and bountiful. They came to Ireland with a fleet of warriors. At the shore, the Tuatha De Danann burned these boats so they could not use them to flee home. They met the Fir Bolg at Moytura. Being a reasonable sort, they offered to share the island. This was not a suggestion that was met with enthusiasm. The only recourse was war, and a terrible battle it was." Glin spoke softly, retelling the legend.

Luci was riveted. It was more dramatic than a soap opera, more magical than a fairy tale.

Suddenly there was a shriek from upstairs and the sound of running footsteps.

"It sounds like Stacey," Jay said.

"That ghost of hers?" Logan asked.

The footsteps came down the front stairs.

"Come back with that, you little . . ."

A second later Tess ran into the library with something in her mouth, followed by Stacey.

Fran and Siobhan raced in. "What's going on?"

"That dog's got it in for me!"

Siobhan caught Tess as she tried to crawl under the sofa. "Bad girl!"

Tess was holding a delicate silk teddy, wagging her tail, pleased with her success. The dog struggled as Siobhan pried her mouth open and extricated the lingerie. Siobhan held it out to Stacey.

"I'm so sorry. We'll replace it, of course."

Stacey took the wrinkled garment. "No need. Just please keep that dog away from me."

Logan grinned. "She likes you, Stacey."

"I don't like her," Stacey replied bluntly, then turned to Tess. "Sorry if that hurts your feelings." She left.

"I really do apologize, Fran," Siobhan said. "We'll keep Tess in the barn from now on. She was locked in the pantry, but she must have found a way out."

"Not to worry." Fran smiled. "At least she has a cheerful personality." Tess was licking Siobhan's face happily. "And now, ladies and gentlemen, it's time we all turned in."

"But, Fran, Glin was just telling us a wonderful story about magic and wizards," Jay protested.

"Was he now? I imagine it's a very old story, if I know Glin, and I'm sure, like so many bards before him, he won't forget how it goes."

Luci was about to ask for another twenty minutes when Fran motioned to the door. "You're outta here."

Luci snuggled into her bed and pulled the covers up around her chin. She could hear the water gurgling over the rocks in the riverbed.

There were no garbage trucks on the street

banging cans. There were no sirens screaming down the avenue. No taxicabs racing across town. No phones ringing in the apartment upstairs. No television next door.

This was heaven.

There was magic in the tales of great warriors and powerful wizards, of beautiful women turning into swans, and of love everlasting.

Luci began to drift off to sleep.

"Are you awake?"

"Umm . . . yes."

"How do you like it here?"

"I love it. It's so peaceful."

"You're kidding, right?"

"If you ignore a couple little things, it's the exact opposite of New York City."

Jay paused. "What about this ghost thing of Stacey's?"

"Huh?"

"Do you believe in ghosts?"

"No."

Jay said nothing.

"Do you?"

"I was walking down the hall to the room this evening and . . . forget it."

"Not likely. What happened?"

"Nothing. At least not that I can put my finger on."

"That's the whole deal with ghosts, isn't it? You can't put your fingers on them." Luci laughed.

"Maybe it was that dog."

"Tess?"

"Maybe she was hiding nearby. I could feel something!"

"Go to sleep, Jay."

"Right."

First thing in the morning, Luci pulled the curtains back and took in the view out the large sliding-glass doors. It wasn't raining, but the mist was hovering low in the valley, giving everything a soft appearance. Almost at the bend in the river, there was a lone fisherman standing thigh-deep in the water. Wearing a beige hat and clothing that matched, he almost disappeared into the background. He swung his arm back and cast his line into the current. Only moments later he began to wind the reel and a trout broke the surface. Expertly, he scooped up the fish in a handheld net.

"He caught one!" Luci exclaimed.

Jay ambled over and stood next to her. "Who is that?"

Luci strained to see, but the mist was too heavy.

Jay opened the door and stepped outside. "It's Logan."

Luci smiled. "Is that his breakfast?"

"What is this?" Stacey poked at a piece of sausage with her fork.

A rosy-faced young woman was serving a breakfast of ham, potatoes, trout, sausage, and toast. There was cold cereal for those who preferred it and Irish oatmeal for those preferring grain in its natural state.

"Black-and-white pudding," Siobhan replied as she poured steaming-hot Irish tea. "It's a traditional breakfast item."

Daria glanced up. "It doesn't look like pudding."

"It's sausage," Fran explained.

"Of course it's sausage. I can see that," Stacey replied. "Why is it so dark?"

Fran paused.

Luci waited for the answer, knowing what Stacey's reaction had to be. She knew that the Scottish meal, haggis, was made with sheep stomach, and she knew what was in black pudding. Which was why she had pushed it to the edge of her plate.

"The . . . uh . . . white pudding is grain and meat," Fran began slowly.

"Yeah," Stacey said suspiciously, then stabbed the sausage with her fork and held it out. "What's in here?"

Fran cleared her throat. "Blood."

"Eek! Augh! Get it off my fork!" Stacey dropped the fork on her plate with a clatter. "I need another fork! I need another plate!"

Logan laughed loudly, doubling up in his chair.

Stacey glared at him. "I don't eat peasant food."

Fran sipped her tea. "Actually, Stacey, you do eat like a peasant. You eat very little meat while concentrating on vegetables."

Stacey pushed her plate away from her and dropped her napkin on top of it.

Logan made a big show of cutting a large piece of blood sausage and popping it into his mouth. "Hmmm."

"Ugh! You're a barbarian!" Stacey said.

Logan raised his eyebrow. "Where I come from that's a compliment, ma'am."

Jay laughed.

Stacey glared at her.

"The trout's wonderful, Logan," Luci commented. "How long did you have to stand in the cold water to catch it?"

"About twenty minutes."

"How about a road trip today?" Fran suggested.

"Great!" Jay responded immediately. "I'd love to see . . . the . . . area. What's there to see?"

"Liam thought we could go bird hunting," Logan replied.

"No no no." Jay shook her head.

"I agree," Luci said. "Let's have a nice drive in the country."

Logan feigned a yawn.

"If we're heading out, I'd like to go to Westport," Glin said.

"What's there?" Daria asked.

"A very famous musician," Glin replied.

"Bono? Is U2 in Westport?" Daria enthused.

"U2 is from Dublin," Aimee offered.

"Where's Dublin from here?" Daria asked.

Luci closed her eyes. "The other side of the country."

"Oh."

"If I can make a suggestion, we can drive around Lough Corrib to Ashford Castle, past Moytura, hit a couple other spots, and have dinner in Westport," Fran suggested.

Everyone nodded in agreement.

"Where am I going to get some Irish woolens?" Stacey asked, ever single-minded.

Chapter Eight

They walked over a small bridge and through the gateway. Ashford Castle stood in front of them. Only a few shades darker gray than the sky, it was immense with crenellations and towers. The wide expanse of manicured, flawless green lawn stretched in all directions, ending only where the turf met the motionless water.

"And I thought River House was big."

"This was built for the Guinness family—"

"The *Book of Records* people?" Daria offered.

"Yes. Except here, they're known more for a kind of beer called stout," Fran replied.

"That black stuff," Stacey said.

"Dark brown," Fran replied.

"They give a bottle every day to the horses at the Irish Stud. It's full of vitamins," Stacey told them.

"And the horses drink it?" Luci asked.

Stacey nodded.

Jay shook her head. "Go figure."

Fran grinned. "Ashford is really not very old,

although it was built on the site of an early Anglo-Norman castle."

"What's Anglo-Norman?" Daria asked.

"Anglo is English. Norman is French," Glin explained. "They were from Normandy and conquered Britain in 1066."

"Isn't Normandy in France?" Daria asked, confused.

"Now. Not then."

"Just take our word for it, Daria. It happened so long ago that these were different people," Jay said impatiently.

"Can we go inside?" Stacey asked.

Fran shook her head. "No. It's a hotel and the interior is for guests only. Tourists can walk around the garden."

"That doesn't seem friendly."

Jay waved her hand at the castle. "This is a showplace. Everyone would be traipsing through. You'd have tour buses lined up at the gate."

Stacey stopped in her tracks. "I don't want to walk in the garden. The grass is wet."

"We'll stay on the walkway. I really want you to see the view of Lough Corrib. It's quite remarkable."

"Why can't we stay someplace like this?" Daria asked as they made their way around the towering gray stone building.

"I want to sleep in a castle," Stacey agreed.

"That would be fun," Luci admitted.

"We'll see. Look at the garden." Fran pointed.

They all glanced. "It's a beautiful garden. Can't you appreciate it just a little? For me?"

"It's soggy," Stacey said.

"It's foggy," Jay added.

"It's cold," Luci chimed in.

"It's Ireland. Why do you think the grass is so green?" Fran replied.

"Spray paint?" Logan asked.

Fran came to a halt. "There's the lake. It's over thirty miles long."

A single rowboat was on the horizon. The rest of the scenery was obscured by the heavy mist.

"Uh-huh," Jay managed.

"All right. Let's go," Fran said dejectedly.

Luci put her arm around Fran's shoulders. "You're doing a fine job."

"Thank you. But I don't believe you for one second."

They completed their circumnavigation of the castle, and Fran referred to the battered map she always carried. "There are many caves in this area. One is called Pigeon Hole. We can walk there. No . . . we can drive there and see the two fairy trout who live inside the cave?"

There was silence.

"Okay. That's a pass on the cave."

"I've had enough caves to last my whole life," Luci stated firmly.

"I don't want fairy trout. I want my trout—" Logan began.

"Right," Jay interrupted. "What else is around here?"

They reached the van and began to climb inside. Aimee beat Stacey to the front seat.

Fran folded the map and placed it on the console. "There's another cave, Captain Webb's Cave. Legend has it he hurled a number of women in and they were never seen again."

Jay groaned.

Fran drove back to the main road. "How about some megalithic remains?"

"I'm for that," Glin replied quickly.

"Sure," Luci agreed. "That's something different."

"Do we have to walk to it?" Stacey asked.

"You're wearing waterproof moccasins," Fran commented.

"And they're giving me blisters."

Fran pointed to the glove box. "Get her the Band-Aids."

Aimee popped the door, found the Band-Aids, and passed them back to Stacey.

"Thank you." Stacey gingerly pulled down her thin socks.

"Gee, Stacey," Luci said as she watched the process. "Those blisters are awful."

Stacey winced as she applied a Band-Aid.

"You should put some antiseptic on those," Glin offered.

Fran stopped at the end of the driveway and turned to glance at Stacey. "We'll take care of it back at the house. No. We'll stop at a pharmacy and pick up some iodine. Can you hang on for a while?"

Stacey nodded.

"Maybe we are walking too much," Fran said.

"We're not at all," Logan replied. "You just need some heavy socks, Stacey."

"Where am I going to get those? At the nearest Saks Fifth Avenue?"

"There are lots of stores in Westport and they have genuine Aran Island sweaters. Okay?" Fran took a right-hand turn. "We'll go to Ballymagibbon Cairn."

They drove along a winding road.

"Oscar Wilde lived in this area when he was a child in Moytura House. It's also on Lough Corrib."

"Who was—" Daria began.

"A famous writer," Luci replied. "He wrote some lovely fairy tales."

Logan grunted.

"As well as *The Picture of Dorian Gray,*" Jay added.

"It was a movie. The painting of Dorian Gray grows younger while the real man ages. Something like that," Jay explained.

Daria shook her head. "I don't get it."

"It's about how we relate to the concept of time," Aimee offered. "It's something that only exists in our minds. If you think of a comb . . ."

Luci widened her eyes and looked at Jay.

Aimee continued. "If you face the comb, that's how we think of time. One tooth following another in sequence. But if you turn the comb the other way, all teeth seem to be one." Aimee smiled. "Time."

Jay nodded.

Minutes later they were in the middle of a field.

"This is it?" Daria asked. "A couple boulders?"

"This is Moytura. The Plain of the Pillar. This is the plain. And this"—Glin pointed to the rocks—"is the pillar."

"What happened here?" Daria asked.

"Some old guys fought each other." Logan grinned.

"It was the fur balls and the tutu danus," Jay replied.

"Fir Bolgs and the Tuatha De Dananns," Glin said.

Jay winked at him. "Oh yeah, them, too."

"Were they from France?" Daria asked.

Everyone said *no*.

"Daria," Fran said. "Just think of it as happening before recorded history."

"That's a long time."

"On this plane," Aimee added. "In another dimension, the battle could be happening around us. And most people would never know."

Luci wondered if some people could know the Tuatha De Dananns were fighting right now? Like Aimee?

She glanced around the field. There was silence. No clash of swords or spears, no shouts from warriors.

Luci shivered.

"Are you okay?" Glin asked.

"Just a chill."

Aimee smiled. "Maybe you were touched by the past."

"Maybe she should have worn her heavy sweater," Jay replied pragmatically.

Fran patted the top stone. "This cairn remains. It tells us something about the people who put it here."

Daria studied the stone marker. "Like . . ."

"That something important happened. Something the people of that era wanted to commemorate. That someone who was very important died on this spot," Glin answered.

"Oh." Daria thought for a long moment. "Who?"

"No one knows," Fran replied. "It was before the written word. It's not like going to Forest Lawn Cemetery to see where Marilyn Monroe is buried."

"I went there," Daria said.

Jay linked her arm through Luci's and headed back to the van. "She has no knowledge of the world outside of California."

"She must know about something."

"We don't have any evidence of that."

"Daria is a good rider."

"Stacey's better."

Luci shrugged. "Stacey's like a ballet dancer. Everything she does is graceful. But Daria is strong."

"That's true. She's looks like she could tip over a cow if she had to."

Stacey was limping back to the van.

"It's that bad, huh?" Luci asked.

Stacey nodded.

"You shouldn't do any more walking," Jay told her.

"I don't want to miss anything," Stacey replied. "I've always wanted to come to Ireland. What am I going to do? Sit in the van while everyone else sees—"

"Rock formations?" Jay laughed.

Stacey smiled. "I guess I could have missed that."

The rest of the group returned to the van.

"Next stop Ballintubber Abbey. It's one of the oldest churches in continual use in all of Europe."

Jay glanced to Stacey.

"Maybe I could miss that."

Westport, or Cathair na Mart in Irish, which translated to Stone Fort of the Cattle, was a small city on Clew Bay. The main street, called the Mall, was situated on the Carrowbeg River. Fran drove over a gray stone bridge and parked so they could do some shopping before the stores closed for the day. There was even a store that featured the crafts of local artisans nearby for Jay to visit.

Luci and Jay examined everything in each store with fascination. There were many tourist items, like linen tea towels with green cottages printed on them. Little china bells embellished with shamrocks. Belleck-porcelain everything. Waterford crystal goblets. Shillelaghs, the traditional Irish walking sticks. There were leprechauns galore. Connemara marble jewelry. Claddagh rings.

Jay tried on a lovely purple wool jacket while Luci pulled on a hand-knit sweater. As they looked at their reflections in the full-length mirror, they laughed. "I don't think either of us would pass as an Irish lass!"

"We could always dye our hair red," Luci replied.

"The craftsmanship is impeccable." Jay studied the garments closely. "My mother would love this jacket."

Luci thought for a moment. "How about a scarf? They come in the same heathery colors."

Jay removed the jacket and moved to the large display of woolen scarfs. "The pink or the purple?"

"The purple. Definitely."

Jay raised the soft wool to her face. "It's heavenly." She held it out for Luci to feel. "I shouldn't splurge."

"Not unless you'll be back in Ireland anytime soon."

"You're right."

They paid for their purchases and went back out to the street to wait for the others. Soon Daria appeared carrying two bulging bags full of presents.

Stacey limped out of a store with her modest acquisitions, having carefully decided upon several beautiful cream-colored wool sweaters and an Irish wool cap for her father. And heavy socks.

In a used-book store, Aimee found an old copy of a volume on Celtic magic. Glin bought a can of dressing for his waxed cotton raincoat and Logan purchased an old navigational map for his father.

Ever practical, Fran window-shopped and nothing more.

They drove to the coast road and on the Quay found the Dulaman, a small restaurant overlooking the water. It was whitewashed inside and out, which made it bright as the evening neared.

As they entered, Luci was struck by the scent of smoke. She sniffed, unable to identify the odor. "What is that?"

Fran pointed to the small fireplace on one wall. "A peat fire."

Luci went to a brass bucket near the hearth. It was full of black bricks. She touched one. It was hard. She picked it up and sniffed it. "Is this peat?"

"Yes."

"It's so hard. Is it peat moss?"

"Compressed. Ireland is full of peat bogs. Peat is a carbonized moss, very very old."

"There's nothing new in Ireland," Daria commented. "Everything is very very old. Before the written record."

"Right. We'll be passing a bog one of these days. They strip-mine it. It's not a very pretty sight, but peat has provided heat for a thousand years."

Luci handed the block of peat to Jay as Logan and Glin pulled a couple tables together near the fire. "The butter tastes like this smells."

Stacey sniffed the peat and wrinkled her nose. "It does."

Fran smiled. "The cows eat the grass which grows on the peat. Of course all the dairy products have a faint taste of peat. It's not bad."

"No," Luci replied quickly. "I like it. I want to bring one of these home. How does one buy these things?"

"Didn't you see them on the street in Oughterard? There was a mound of them in front of a store.

We'll stop someplace and you can stock up, I promise."

Luci grinned as she slipped into a chair by the wall and Glin sat next to her.

A cheery woman approached with handwritten menus. "Good evening. Here for dinner? Everything is fresh. I made it all myself this afternoon."

"Sounds wonderful." Luci began to study the menu.

Glin looked up. "I heard that Finn Lunny comes in here."

The woman smiled. "That he does. He's great friends with Matt Molloy."

"Of the Chieftains?" Glin asked.

"You've heard of them. The boys are very popular here, but I didn't know they were well-known in America."

Fran nodded. "Especially on St. Patrick's Day!"

The woman laughed. "That's your holiday, isn't it? As for Finn Lunny, he doesn't live here in Westport. He's up in Donegal. What town did he say? My memory isn't what it used to be. Are you looking for Finn, then?"

"I'd like to meet him," Glin admitted.

"His father has a pub. Find him and you'll find Finn."

The woman left to answer the phone.

"Donegal?" Fran asked.

Luci and Jay raised their hands immediately. Aimee followed, then Stacey. Logan and Daria held out.

"I want to go hunting," Daria said.

"You can do that, too," Fran assured her.

Daria raised her hand.

Everyone turned to Logan.

"Okay, okay." He raised his hand.

"Terrific. We all agree—for once!" Fran sighed.

Chapter Nine

Luci managed to mount her horse without any help and that pleased her. She settled herself in the saddle and squared the hard hat on her head.

Next to her Jay was struggling with the reins. On one side, the leather was caught on the bit and she couldn't quite reach it from the saddle without falling to the ground.

Logan urged his horse forward and easily leaned over and freed the rein. "Okay?"

"Yes, thank you."

Standing slightly in the saddle, Luci lifted her oversized sweater so she wouldn't be sitting on it.

"Are we ready?" Liam asked.

Fran checked the group one more time. "I think we are. Aimee, how are you?"

Aimee didn't answer.

"Aimee!" Fran waved her hand at her.

Aimee looked up. "Yes?"

"Are you wearing earphones again?"

"No."

"Then why didn't you hear me?"

"I was aligning myself with the horse."

"Are you finished?"

Aimee nodded.

"Then we're ready."

The group moved off down the driveway.

"I thought we'd take a nice walk this morning through the hills," Siobhan remarked. "There's a view of the river that's simply magnificent."

"Walk?" Logan asked contemptuously.

"You don't have to do everything at full speed," Fran told him. "You might miss something."

Logan appeared unconvinced.

They rode on till the driveway ended and Liam opened a gate into a field. The terrain was somewhat uneven and began to slope upward.

"We are going to be spending a couple days up north," Fran told Siobhan. "Glin's looking for someone in Donegal."

"How nice. I know a wonderful place for you to stay if you want to do something the Irish do," Siobhan replied.

"Yes!" Luci answered quickly.

Fran laughed. "You don't even know what it is."

"That's okay. I don't want to be so much of a tourist gawking at everything. I could stay at home and watch travel videos. I want to participate."

"Me, too. We're doing too much sightseeing," Jay added.

"I agree," Stacey added.

Luci looked at her. She never expected Stacey to

concur with anything the rest of them said or wanted to do.

"If you don't want to gawk at the scenery, why don't we stay here and do everything River House offers?" Logan asked.

Jay was reaching down trying to turn her stirrup iron around so the leather would be flat against her leg. "Not all of us want to ride all day long, every day."

"We haven't even gone hiking yet," Logan reminded her.

Liam smiled. "I thought we might do that this afternoon."

"Great!"

Luci sighed.

"Then we can go to Donegal tomorrow," Fran said.

"But there's a hunt tomorrow," Logan objected.

"Fran . . . I want to go hunting," Daria protested. "This is the real thing."

"Okay, okay. How about if we leave after the hunt?"

Logan nodded.

"That'll mean we won't make it to Donegal by evening, though," Fran said.

Siobhan smiled. "There's a place in Ballina you could stay. It's very picturesque. It's called Ballina Castle."

"Is it a real castle?" Stacey asked.

"Oh yes."

"They have quite a collection of armor, which I'm sure would interest you, Logan," Liam offered.

"Let's do that," Glin said.

Luci turned to Aimee. "You want to stay in a castle tomorrow night?"

"Sure."

They continued up the hill. There was a low stone wall in their path.

"Anyone want to jump the wall?" Liam asked.

"No!" Luci replied. She could stay on at a trot and canter, provided everything was perfect, but she wasn't going to test her luck by jumping something.

Siobhan, Fran, Jay, Luci, and Aimee headed for the edge of the field, where there was a break in the wall. Luci turned back and could see the others galloping up the hill and easily jumping over the wall.

"I feel like a klutz," Luci admitted. "Look at Stacey."

"She *is* a beautiful rider," Siobhan conceded.

The other group pulled up and waited for the stragglers.

"Stacey must have been practicing most of her life to be that proper," Siobhan continued.

Luci didn't doubt it for a minute. Stacey wasn't the kind of person who would waste her time doing something halfway, whether it was her hair, her clothing, or her riding.

They caught up with the others and Glin fell into step with Luci. "How are you doing?"

"Fine."

"Is your horse giving you any trouble?"

"No."

Just then the horse tried to put his head down and

grab a mouthful of grass. Luci was pulled forward out of the saddle and practically smashed her nose on his neck.

"Except he keeps trying to eat." Luci laughed.

"Try to catch him before he does that. Once he's got the full weight of his head going down, you're lost."

"A horse's head and neck weigh about three hundred pounds," Logan declared.

"I don't want to know how you know that," Jay remarked.

"Then I won't tell you." Logan grinned. "Hey, Glin, remember when we were up back of that other farm and the hounds got on the . . ."

Glin shook his head.

Luci looked from Glin to Logan and back again.

"You remember," Logan insisted. "The hounds were barking and the whips couldn't move them from under the tree."

Glin was shaking his head more emphatically.

"What happened?" Jay asked.

Before Logan could answer, Glin jumped in. "Nothing."

"What are you talking about? The hounds got on the—"

"Nothing!" Glin said pointedly.

"What happened?" Stacey asked.

"You weren't there. We were with the master and the first field," Logan explained.

"What happened?" Stacey repeated.

"You don't have to know. Nothing happened," Glin said.

Stacey pulled her horse to a halt. "You're talking to someone who has hunted before. What happened?"

Everyone had to stop, because Stacey refused to move.

Logan and Glin looked at each other. Liam was checking his horse's mane very carefully.

"If Glin says nothing happened," Fran said, "why don't we just believe him and have a nice ride?"

"I don't like people keeping things from me," Stacey said firmly.

"You know," Luci said, "I don't either. If something happened, I think it should be shared."

"Are you men trying to protect us?" Jay asked. The way she said it made it sound like a very bad idea. "You wouldn't demean us in that way, would you? You wouldn't deprive us of important knowledge which might help us make informed decisions. Would you?" She glared at them.

"Glin . . ." Luci began.

"All right, all right. It was out back of this farm; the hounds went down this lane. Half the field was up on the hill. We heard this . . . meow-meow."

"The hounds got on a cat?" Stacey asked horrified.

"Yes," Logan replied, glaring at her.

"They didn't get on the cat. The cat was up the tree. No harm came to the cat," Glin assured them.

"I don't believe you," Stacey replied.

"It's true," Liam concurred.

"The cat wasn't hurt. It was scared, that's about all."

"So let me review this. Twenty-five big smelly hounds chase a little, tiny, defenseless cat up a tree," Jay said.

"Yeah. See? No big deal." Logan urged his horse forward.

Jay looked at Luci. The disgust on her face was obvious.

"They're hunting dogs. It's instinct," Logan stated without turning around. "That's what they're trained to do."

"That's a pack out of control!" Stacey shouted.

The ride continued in silence.

They returned to the barn and Stacey was the first to finish untacking her horse. Without a word, she went back to the house.

"What's the matter with her?" Logan asked.

Luci sighed.

"Let me give you some advice, Logan," Fran said. "Do not say another word about hunting while in Stacey's presence."

"Why would I accommodate her?"

Glin looked at Logan in amazement. "Because we all have to live together."

Luci and Jay walked the house and went to their room.

"We have to do something about this," Jay declared.

Luci washed her face. "Like?"

"Suggest something."

"Why put this all on me? I'm a city girl. I know nothing about hunting or horses or hounds. We never even had a cat. You have a brother. I don't even have one of those. How about putting some strapping tape over Logan's mouth?"

"I don't think that'll work."

"We're going to Donegal tomorrow."

"Not before they go hunting." Jay plopped herself on the edge of the bed. "Tell Glin to tell Logan not to go hunting."

Luci stepped out of the bathroom. "I can't do that."

"You're right. You can't," Jay admitted, standing up and going to the door. "I'll tell him myself!"

Luci rushed after her. "You can't give Logan orders. You'll just make him more obstinate."

"First it's a cat—who got lucky. Then it's the fox who isn't going up a tree. What's next? Those protesters have a point. The whole dirty business should be banned!"

Luci agreed. She just didn't know what they could do about it.

The mood of the group was not improved by a lunch of cream-of-carrot soup and hearty sandwiches on whole-grain bread. Stacey wouldn't eat the soup and only picked at her sandwich. Jay wouldn't eat anything. Daria and Logan were the only ones whose appetites were unaffected by the conflict.

"People," Fran began. "Eat lunch. I don't want to be on the road and have to deal with hunger pangs."

"I'm not going," Stacey returned.

"We all agreed this morning we'd go to Galway this afternoon," Daria told her.

Stacey glared. "That was then. This is now."

"Let's put all this behind us and have a nice day."

"I'm not preventing anyone from doing anything. I'm just not going along with you."

Luci was convinced. Stacey wasn't susceptible to sweet-talking, cajoling, or reason. No meant no.

At that moment Luci felt a wave of admiration for Stacey. She hoped one day she could be as decisive and unmovable, but Luci could always be persuaded to give in if someone begged hard enough.

"Let her stay here," Logan replied.

"We're a group," Glin pointed out. "We're here to do things together."

"We haven't signed a contract," Logan said. "The rest of us want to go to Galway. Who cares if she stays here?"

Luci looked up. "I care."

"Me, too," Jay added. "I'll stay here."

Fran put her hands over her face. "Guys. You're killing me. I'm supposed to show you Ireland. I'm supposed to provide a positive experience for you. This is my job. If I don't do it well, I won't have it anymore."

Stacey stood up. "This has nothing to do with you and I will be more than happy to write a letter to Getaway Tours to that effect." She left the room.

"Wow," Luci whispered to herself. That was a girl who knew her own mind. And it was a little frightening.

"Fine. Are we ready to go now?" Logan asked.

Jay stood. "You're so insensitive," she told him, and left the room.

Everyone looked at Luci, waiting for her to do something.

"I'll stay. You go and have fun. We'll be okay."

"We're going to talk about this. I want this—whatever it is—resolved before it goes any further," Fran said.

Glin hung back to be with Luci as the group left the dining room. "Do you want me to stay here with you?"

"You don't have to do that, but thanks."

"Things will be better tomorrow."

Luci nodded. "I'm sure of it."

Chapter Ten

Luci and Jay watched the van go down the driveway. A moment later Stacey came out of the house wearing a jacket and walking shoes.

"Where are you going?" Luci asked.

"Town."

"You're walking?" Jay asked in amazement.

"That seems to be the only way to get there."

"There's nothing in town. No boutiques. No movies. Why would you walk all the way to town?" Luci asked.

"Maybe I can find that woman."

Jay was confused. "Which one?"

"That animal-rights woman," Stacey replied impatiently.

"Do you mind if I go with you?" Luci asked.

Stacey, Luci, and Jay reached the town square and studied their surroundings. There was very little traffic and no one walking who might be able to offer directions or information.

"What makes you think she lives in town? Maybe she lives as far away as Ballyconneely or Clifden."

"Then we'll call her and have her meet us here," Stacey replied logically.

"What if she doesn't have a phone?" Jay asked. "Not everyone does here."

Fran had pointed out the lone phone booths by the roadside in some of the towns they had driven through. That one telephone would serve the entire population.

Stacey marched to the entrance of Humanity Dick's pub. "We'll find out and deal with it." She opened the door.

"What if we're not allowed inside? In America you can't go into a bar at our age," Luci pointed out at the threshold.

"Then stand out on the street," Stacey retorted as she went into the pub.

Jay and Luci waited for a moment, expecting Stacey to be tossed out by the bartender as he threatened to call the police. When nothing happened, they followed her inside.

There was a man behind the bar stocking a shelf with clean glasses.

"Excuse me," Stacey said, walking up to the bar. "We're looking for Ethne Coughlin."

The bartender turned to her and grinned. "Are you now? You've not far to go." He pointed with his towel.

In a corner of the room the gray-haired woman was having a late lunch.

"Ethne," the man called out. "You have some visitors."

Stacey walked directly to the table.

Ethne closed her newspaper. "May I help you?"

"I think the question is, can I help you?" Stacey responded.

Ethne motioned for the girls to sit and asked for another pot of tea. "You're the American tourists."

Luci nodded. "We're not here to make trouble, but we don't feel right about the hunt."

The man brought some tea and a plate of biscuits.

"Then you have character," Ethne replied as she poured tea for each of them. "Foxhunting may have had a purpose in the past, but it has no place in a modern, humane society."

"Shouldn't you work to get it outlawed?" Luci asked.

"Not enough people care. And it's a tradition. We hold to our heritage very tightly even when it's wrong."

"Couldn't you talk to Brendan? Come to some agreement?"

Ethne smiled sadly. "You don't know him. He's not one to listen. He makes his mind up and he sees it as a moral weakness to change it."

"Why do men have to be like that?" Jay sighed.

"Not all of them," Luci replied. "My father's not like that. He's reasonable."

"Brendan comes from a military background. His father, his father's father. Compromise is defeat."

"This isn't a contest," Luci said. "Or a war. You're not trying to win for personal gain."

Ethne sipped her tea. "Years ago, many years ago, Brendan and I were in love. We were to be married. But there was a war in Europe and everyone was swept up by the fighting. I wanted to do my part, too. I didn't want to stay home and fold bandages for the Red Cross. My father had been the editor of the newspaper in Galway and I had some experience as a photographer for him. It seemed to me that I could go to the front and, using my camera, show the world what was happening. If you show people the truth, they'll make the right choices."

"Did you go?" Luci asked.

"I did, and I wasn't shy about it. My photos ran on the front page of *The London Times* and soon I had made a name for myself and everyone knew of me. I went where few other journalists did, and certainly no women. Against Brendan's wishes. He said it was no place for a woman, his fiancée. He said if I continued, our engagement was off. I didn't believe him. He was true to his word."

Luci felt tears come to her eyes. "That's so sad."

"A waste, I will admit," Ethne agreed.

Stacey put her hands down on the table. "All right. So it's no use trying to come to an understanding with him."

"I'm afraid not."

"That's why you've been protesting," Luci said. "That's the only choice left open to you."

"But what good does it do to protest?" Jay asked. "If you're reaching such a very small audience . . ."

"Your public relations need to be upgraded," Stacey said reasonably. "You need to increase public awareness. Get them involved. Tell them exactly what's going on. Elicit their compassion."

"And how would I do that?"

"Contact the media. Television. Newspapers. Send out press releases. Sway public opinion to your side. Put the pressure on the opposition. One person is easy to ignore. You can be dismissed as a troublesome kook. But when your side becomes the majority, they won't be able to oppose you."

Luci watched Stacey as she spoke. She had it all figured out. Stacey was like a guided missile seeking its target. There was no question in her mind what had to be done and how to go about doing it. She exuded confidence.

"This isn't America," Ethne said. "We don't have the outlets you do. Or even what is available in Dublin. In Ballynahinch we receive two television channels, and one of them is CNN."

"We'll just have to work harder," Jay replied firmly.

Ethne smiled. "I never turn away from a helping hand. But will we have time to do anything before tomorrow?"

"We'll make time," Luci said.

Luci was standing on a hill. Down below her were the hunters. Suddenly a fox darted out of a burrow and began to run across the field.

"Help!"

Luci tried to run down the hill, but it seemed as if her legs weighed a ton.

"Help!"

She was ankle-deep in a peat bog and sinking fast.

"Help!" someone was shouting. Who was it?

"Luci!"

Jay was shaking her. "Wake up!"

She opened her eyes. "Huh?"

"Stacey's ghost!"

"Help!"

Jay pulled on her robe and raced out of the room.

Luci wanted to roll over and go back to sleep. But not to go back to that dream.

There was shouting. Tess began barking.

Luci sat up. It sounded too good to miss. She threw back the covers, grabbed her robe, and dashed out of the room.

Upstairs in the hallway, Daria was nearly hysterical. She kept pointing to the room and making pressing motions with her hands.

Stacey stood by without saying a word.

"I'll go make her some chamomile tea," Siobhan said, and rushed down the stairs as Luci was going up.

"What's the matter with you women?" Logan asked. "We changed rooms with you. We haven't had any problems. Go back to sleep!" He went into his room and slammed the door.

"It was the ghost," Daria insisted. "It pushed on the edge of my bed and then it lay down right next to me!"

"What!" Jay gasped.

"I could feel it!"

Stacey was holding back a smirk.

"Was it warm?" Glin asked.

"No, it wasn't warm!"

Fran put her arm around Daria's shoulder. "Let's go have a cup of tea."

"Where am I going to sleep?" Daria wailed. "How are you going to keep the ghost from attacking me?"

"There are no ghosts!" Logan bellowed from behind his closed door.

"It's one thing to have it walking around and rattling chains, but when it's crawling into bed with you . . ." Daria began to cry as Fran helped her downstairs.

"Well . . ." Jay said.

Stacey finger-combed her hair into place. "I told you."

Luci nodded. "You want our room?"

"There are twenty rooms up here; we don't have to make you move."

"Where's Aimee?"

They looked around.

"Maybe she slept through it," Jay suggested.

"Good for her if she could do that," Glin replied.

Luci was unsure. "Should we wake her up?"

"Why?" Glin asked.

"She's the only one who knows anything about—"

"Oh, be serious," Stacey said. "Do you know who her mother is?"

"No."

"Alis Acacia. She's so far out you need a satellite uplink to talk to her. Sedona, Arizona, is a magnet for the weirdos of the world."

"I thought that was L.A.," Glin commented.

"We get our share, I won't argue that. But Sedona is in red-rock country. The New Agers say there's a special vibration. Healing, channeling—it's all magnified there. That's why Alis Acacia moved to Sedona. It was for business. How do you think Aimee affords all these trips?"

"I didn't think about it," Jay admitted.

"It's from all these psychic readings her mother gives. She's like the high priestess of it," Stacey said.

Luci tried to picture Aimee's mother. Did she wear long flowing dresses? Did she wear black like Aimee? Did she cast spells? Did she worship the moon skyclad? "Does that mean it's not true?" Luci asked.

"What do you think?"

"I don't know," Luci replied. She had always wondered if it was possible to predict the future. It was strange enough to be real.

"Tch." Stacey shook her head and went back to her room.

"It could be true," Luci countered.

Glin nodded.

"You don't think it is."

"It could be. People have believed in prophets for thousand of years. Maybe Aimee's mother is one of them," Glin agreed.

Jay tapped on Aimee's door. "Are you awake?"

"Sure. Come on in."

Jay opened the door and motioned for the others.

"Daria says the ghost was sitting on her bed."

"I know."

"You heard her screaming."

"No. The ghost told me."

Chapter Eleven

"**W**hat do you mean the ghost told you?" Jay asked.

Luci wasn't sure she wanted to know.

Aimee smiled. "It came to me and said it was looking for something."

"Like . . ."

"That's when you knocked."

"How did it come to you?" Jay asked.

"Did you see it?" Luci asked.

"What else did it say?" Glin asked.

"It didn't say what it was looking for. I couldn't see it."

"Could you feel it?"

"I could feel its presence."

"Did it press on the end of your bed?" Luci wondered.

"No."

Glin shrugged. "That doesn't give us much to go on."

"Do you believe it?" Jay asked.

"Three people have experienced this ghost so far. Are all of them wrong?"

"Maybe all of them were asleep. I read about this sleep-paralysis thing. You're asleep but you think you're awake. . . ."

"No," Luci corrected. "You're asleep, but then you wake up but you can't move."

"And that's when you're abducted by extraterrestrials," Jay finished.

"Let's not add to this," Glin suggested. "Ghosts are enough for now."

"Ask him what he wants," Luci told Aimee.

"It's gone now."

"Is it a girl ghost or a guy ghost?" Jay wanted to know.

Aimee shook her head.

Glin headed for the door. "I think we should all turn in and see if we can forget about this. We won't be here for a couple of nights and maybe it'll all go away."

Luci nodded.

"It's just so strange," Jay commented.

"Not at all," Aimee replied as she lay back down.

They closed the door behind them. Downstairs the hall clock chimed two.

"Good night, ladies."

"Night, Glin," Luci responded.

"We must be crazy."

Luci was shivering in her raincoat, the heavy mist falling around them so determinedly that it might as well be rain.

Jay had found hats for them both. Hers was yellow rubberized material so old it was probably older than her mother. It was so large, it fell down over her eyes.

Luci's was a green waxed cotton cap that was long past due for another waxing. Her fingers were turning blue and her toes were cold. "We're standing out in the middle of a big field waiting for something that might never happen."

Jay shook her head and the hat fell over her eyes again. She pushed it back. "Ethne knows the terrain. If she says the hunt will come out this way, then it will."

"How are we going to stop fifty running horses? This is a really dumb idea."

Jay held up a horn. "We toot this."

"Then twenty-five hounds run us down instead of the fox."

"Ethne said she'd get here before the hunt did."

Luci nodded, not believing any of it.

"Why are you so cranky this morning?"

"Sleep deprivation! I haven't had a good night's sleep since we got here. Every time I settle in, Stacey or Daria starts shouting. Someone should stuff a sock in their mouths."

"You may be the next one who the ghost fancies."

"Please. Please. You don't believe that, do you?"

"In ghosts?"

"Yes."

"In school we read a story by a French writer,

Guy de Maupassant. The same thing happened. A ghost came and pressed on the bottom of the bed and woke the sleeper. It was called the Horla."

"That's hardly proof," Luci commented.

Jay pushed the hat back. "The story was written a hundred years ago. Is it coincidence that the same circumstances occur both here and in the story?"

"Yeah."

Jay shifted her weight from one foot to the other and back again, trying to keep warm. "I just hope the ghost picks you next."

"Jay!"

"I didn't mean it as bad as it came out."

"I hope not."

They both scanned the hills for any sign of life.

"I'll be so glad to get away from here for a couple days."

Luci sighed. "Me, too. And I feel so bad that I can say that after spending my whole life wanting to travel, wanting to stay in a beautiful house. Isn't this a gorgeous place?"

"Fantastic."

"It's like being in an Emily Brontë book. The sky is in turmoil with dark clouds and mist. The hills are unspoiled and stretch away to the horizon. It's wild and primitive and we're not enjoying it. That makes me mad!"

"Between ghosts and becoming political activists we haven't had a moment's peace," Jay agreed.

"Let's go back to the house."

"We can't leave now. Ethne is counting on us."

"How'd we get roped into this?"

"It seemed like a good idea to save the life of this fox."

"This week. We're here. We save it this week. What happens when we go? Who protects it then?" Luci stamped her feet to keep warm.

Jay had been thinking the same thing.

The mist changed to rain.

Luci could feel her head getting wet. Her toes were numb. "I'm going back. I don't want to get pneumonia just to make a statement."

"Maybe you're right. There's no guarantee they'll come this way."

They began walking back.

"What's that?" Jay stopped and listened.

"The wind."

"No. I think it's the hounds."

"It's your imagination." All Luci could hear was the rain pelting on her cap.

They began walking again, eyes down, trying to avoid tripping on rocks or falling into a hole.

Jay stopped. "There is it again."

Luci looked up and scanned the field.

Jay pointed. "Over there!"

Luci strained her eyes to see through the mist and rain. "It's the fox!"

"It's running this way!"

"What do we do? What do we do!"

Luci grabbed onto Jay. Jay grabbed onto Luci. "Run!"

"Which way?"

There wasn't a tree to climb or a rock to hide behind.

The fox was running straight up the hill, directly toward them.

The baying of the hounds grew louder.

"Luci . . ."

"Jay . . ."

Jay tugged Luci's arm and began running across the top of the hill. Her hat fell down over her eyes and Jay pushed it as they ran.

Luci glanced back. The fox was still headed in their direction. She could see the hounds far down the field.

"We can't outrun the dogs!"

"I could toot the horn."

"Can you toot S-T-O-P? Or are you just going to be blowing what amounts to here we are come and get it?"

"Sorry. I don't know the equivalent of Morse code for hounds and horn."

The baying was getting louder. Horns were blowing in the distance.

"They're all coming now!"

"Where are we going?"

"Like I know?"

"I thought you might have a plan."

"I do! Keep running!"

Luci turned her head. The hounds were gaining on them. She could see the horses and riders following not far behind.

Jay pulled Luci's arm and dragged her down a slope. They began sliding on the wet grass. In a tumble of arms and legs, they both went down, rolling, bumping downward, landing face forward.

Luci spit out a mouthful of dirt and grass. There was a moment of silence. "Maybe they've gone the other way."

A second later the baying was almost on top of them.

Luci jumped to her feet, grabbed Jay, and began running again.

Jay turned. The hounds were close. The riders not far behind.

"Come on!" Luci shouted.

"Maybe if we just stand our ground. We *are* humans. They're not going to hurt us." It was more a question than a statement.

"If you believe that, you stay," Luci said.

Jay watched in horror as the hounds drew closer. "You're right!"

A moment later they were surrounded by hounds with open mouths and big teeth.

There was a shot. Then silence. The report echoed in the hills.

Luci turned. Ethne was standing next to a Land Rover, gun in hand pointed to the sky.

"Get in the car."

Luci and Jay pushed through the pack of hounds toward the vehicle.

The horses raced up the hill and stopped. The master glared. The huntsmen worked the hounds away from the car. The rest of the field halted nearby.

Brendan was furious. "Ethne! Have you taken leave of your senses? This has gone too far!"

Fran pulled her horse to a halt alongside Logan and Glin. She was not smiling.

Chapter Twelve

In the town square, Stacey was coordinating the media. There was a television van, lights set up, video-camera operators, reporters, and still photographers.

Ethne halted the four-wheel-drive vehicle next to Stacey and Luci rolled down the window. "You'd better come back."

"Not now. We haven't had the interviews. Ethne, please. They want to talk to you."

Ethne shut off the engine and got out.

Lights were trained on her. The reporters gathered, pushing microphones and microcassette recorders toward her.

Ethne cleared her throat. "Foxhunting is a mistake. But it's a mistake to put people in harm's way, too. I will continue to fight this inhumanity, but will do it alone. I can't risk the safety of people who are only seeking to protect the defenseless among us." She turned away.

"One question!"

"Please. Miss Coughlin! What happened in the field?"

"Is this going to put an end to the protest?"

"Are you willing to concede defeat?"

Ethne didn't say another word; she just got back in the car and drove the girls back to River House.

Fran glared at them. "I'm at a loss for words."

Luci couldn't even look at her.

"I know I can't trust Logan."

"Excuse me," Logan replied indignantly.

"We all know what you're like," Fran said. "It's not an insult. But I thought Luci and Jay were responsible. And I never thought Stacey would be involved in orchestrating a media circus."

"It worked," Stacey responded. "We got the publicity."

"Luci and Jay could have been very badly hurt. Being on foot in the hunt field is extremely dangerous."

"Are you going to tar and feather them?" Logan asked.

"Everyone else go pack. I want you all in the van in five minutes, sitting with your hands folded, eyes forward."

"Fran . . ." Glin started.

"Go!"

Everyone left the blue room.

"What do you think I should do with you?"

Stacey regarded her evenly. "Nothing. We stopped the hunt. We were successful in raising public awareness. Goal achieved."

"You're missing the point."

"I doubt it."

"Stacey, what you did was wrong."

"What they're doing is wrong."

"That's not for you to say."

"Of course it is. Do you know the Eleventh Commandment?"

Luci and Jay exchanged a confused glance.

Fran shook her head.

"Thou shalt not stand idly by."

Fran raised her hands. "I don't want to get into politics. We're on a tour. We are guests in this country. You cannot become instigators. You cannot become some kind of animal-rights terrorists."

"We are guests on this planet," Stacey said. "All of us, from the littlest creature to the biggest."

Jay couldn't believe what she was hearing.

"I agree," Luci said.

Fran nodded, sighing. "I do, too. But the three of you were completely out of line this morning and behaved recklessly. For the rest of our stay I want you to have no more to do with foxhunting or that woman in town. Understand?"

Luci nodded.

"Get packed. We're late."

For most of the trip the tourists had been silent. Glin and Logan kept a conversation going between themselves, talking of experiences he had had in Montana. Luci had been lost in thought. Aimee had listened to her music. It was growing dark as the van drove over the River Moy and soon Ballina Castle was in sight.

"Is that it?" Daria asked in awe.

"Yes," Fran replied.

"It's fabulous!"

"It's much smaller than Ashford Castle," Stacey commented.

"It'll be intimate," Fran countered.

"We'll be on top of each other."

"Hardly," Fran said. "I booked lovely big rooms."

"Is the commode in the room or down the hall someplace?" Stacey asked.

"Yeah," Logan interrupted. "Are there indoor facilities?"

Fran drove underneath the large stone archway at the bottom of the drive. "Indoor facilities, in the rooms. It's going to be great."

Luci stared out the window. Banners and flags were hung from the front of the castle, which was lit by an array of lights. The effect was dramatic and spectacular.

"We're really staying here?" Jay asked.

"Yup. Is everyone happy?"

They all agreed it was perfect and more than they could have hoped for.

Fran parked and they all leaped out, scrambling to get their bags so they could see the inside.

"We have to get pictures of this," Luci told Jay as they hurried to the front door.

"Definitely. My mother will not believe this!"

"Fit for a princess," Glin said as he came up behind them.

"Are people going to be dressed in costumes?" Daria asked.

"Why would they do that?"

"They do it in Disneyland. . . ."

Luci sighed.

Stacey paused to stare at Daria. "This isn't a theme park!"

Daria shrugged. "You never know."

"Good luck," Jay muttered under her breath.

Logan pulled the huge wooden door open and the girls stepped through into the foyer.

Luci caught her breath. It was like walking through a time warp and winding up in a medieval castle.

The ceiling was twenty feet up, and made of dark, carved paneled wood. The floor was uneven stone. The fireplace was immense, so large that Luci could almost have walked into it if it hadn't been filled with incredible blazing tree trunks.

There was a staircase with an ornate wooden banister that made a right-hand turn halfway up. On the landing was an urn big enough to hold a person.

Logan walked right over to a full suit of armor that was positioned near the staircase. "And there's a whole museum of this stuff?"

Fran nodded. "That's what Liam says."

"Outstanding."

A young man entered the foyer. "Good evening. You must be the Getaway Tour."

"Yes, we are."

"Lovely. You're in time for dinner. Would you

like to be shown your rooms first or eat first? I can keep your bags behind the desk."

"I'm starving, Fran," Daria whispered.

"I don't have to go upstairs," Luci said.

"Me, neither," Jay agreed.

"Okay, we'll eat and then go upstairs."

"Lovely," the young man replied as he began walking toward the dining room. "Follow me."

They wound their way past a piano bar and into a cozy dining room paneled in dark wood and decorated with colorful banners.

"This is beautiful," Luci said. "Thank you, Fran."

Fran smiled. "I finally did something right."

Logan put his arm around her shoulders. "Don't get a complex on us. You always do a good job."

"Thank you, Logan."

They were shown to a banquette-style table, with a hardwood bench next to the wall and chairs on the opposite side. Glin slid onto the bench. Luci hesitated until Jay gave her a firm push. Luci slid in next to him and Jay followed her. Logan pulled up a chair next to her and Stacey found a place beside him. Daria, Aimee, and Fran filled out the rest of the spots.

"Do you miss Tim?" Luci asked out of the blue, referring to Fran's husband, who had accompanied them on their trip to France.

"No," Fran replied.

"Really?" Jay asked in amazement.

"What I mean is that the great thing about being married to a photographer is that sometimes we spend a lot of time together, and just about the time

when we both need a break from all that together-
ness, he gets an assignment to go off to a shoot."

Logan was engrossed in examining everything on
the table. He tipped over the saltshaker to look at
the bottom. "And where is he this time?"

"New Zealand. He's photographing some scien-
tists who are working with whales."

Fran raised her water glass. *"Slainte."*

The others raised their glasses to toast their
health. *"Slainte."*

They laughed as they tried to pronounce the Irish
word.

Luci studied the menu and made her decision. If
the food was half as good as the rest of the place,
this would be one of the most memorable nights of
her life.

The waiter was clearing the dinner plates. "How
was your meal?"

Fran smiled. *"Bhi an beile go brea, go raibh
maith agat."*

"An bhfuill Gaeilge agat?"

"Ta, beagainin."

"Because you speak a little Irish, dessert is our
treat."

"Go raibh maith agat," Fran replied. "Thank you
very much."

"May I recommend the trifle? It's a house spe-
cialty."

Luci nodded. "All right."

"Trifle all around?" the waiter asked.

Everyone shrugged or nodded in confusion.

"What's trifle?" Daria asked.

Fran held out her hand toward Luci.

"Trifle is a traditional English dessert made of layers of sponge cake, custard, and jam. Maybe some fresh berries."

"Fat," Stacey said.

"Yup," Fran replied as the waiter returned and began placing dishes in front of them. "Lots and lots of clotted cream."

"I'm sure you'll love it," he told them, then left.

Luci studied the contents of the dish. It definitely was not what she had imagined or in fact had ever had before.

Daria poked at the dessert with her spoon. "What's this?"

Jay put a red cube on her spoon and held it up to the dim light. "Jell-O?"

It was a mess. There were no layers. The cake and the cream and the Jell-O were all mixed together. This wasn't right.

"Is this supposed to be in here?" Jay asked, holding the spoon out to Luci.

"Why are you blaming me? I just told you what *normally* is in a trifle."

Fran took a spoonful of dessert. "Maybe Irish trifle is different."

Stacey regarded the glass suspiciously. "Different all right."

"Just eat it."

Stacey shook her head.

Daria pushed hers away. "I don't like Jell-O. It's so rubbery."

Jay put down her spoon. "The cake is stale."

Luci shrugged. "Yeah. There's not much point. . . ."

The waiter returned. "It's a lovely dessert, isn't it?"

They all nodded and picked up their spoons.

"Do we get a reward for belonging to the Clean Plate Club?" Luci asked as they went up the stairs to their rooms.

"It was gross," Jay whispered.

"Don't think about it," Luci told her.

"I thought it was fine," Logan said. He had eaten Stacey's portion as well as his own.

"Coming from the man who ate blood sausage, that's not much of a recommendation," Stacey commented dryly.

They went through a fire door into a narrow, dimly lit hall. Luci looked at the key in her hand. Room 14. She stopped at the door and pushed the key into the lock.

"Do you think there will be four-poster beds?" Daria asked hopefully.

"We'll soon see," Fran replied.

Luci pushed open the door and gasped.

Chapter Thirteen

There was a red-fringed shade on the ceiling light and several garish art prints hung from ties on the walls. The room could hardly have been smaller. Two beds were squeezed together with barely enough room to walk around them. To the left there was a tiny bathroom. It was so small, it didn't have a regular hanging door; it had a sliding, pocket door. The paint was chipped.

Everything was old, worn, and dingy.

Except for the shag carpet, which was a vibrant, pulsating red.

From down the hall, Luci could hear Stacey's voice. "It looks like a brothel."

Luci didn't want to go inside.

Jay was stunned.

Luci turned and looked for Fran, who had disappeared.

"It this for real?"

"I think so."

"Fran!" Stacey shouted. "I'm not staying in this

room. What am I supposed to do? Sleep standing up?"

"Are you women bellyaching again?" Logan asked as he stuck his head out the door. "All you need is a bed. Lay down. Go to sleep. We're leaving early in the morning."

"Why don't you take your bedroll, Buffalo Bill, and sleep under the van?" Stacey shot back.

"Because I don't have a problem with the room," Logan retorted, and shut the door.

A moment later the door opened and Glin came out. He walked over to Luci and peered into her room. "Ours isn't any better or we could trade."

Luci went into the room and put down her bag. "Oh, it's okay," she said, but didn't sound convincing.

Jay sat on the bed, which nearly collapsed under her. She lay down. "This is going to be like sleeping in a ditch. I can feel the box spring through the mattress."

Glin took Luci's hand. "I'm sorry."

"It'll be fine."

"I wanted it to be nice for you. And it's like a set from a bad drive-in movie."

Fran came to the doorway. "Okay, Glin. Everyone back to their rooms."

Glin gave Luci's hand a small squeeze then dropped it.

Fran stepped out of the way so he could get through the narrow doorway. "No boys in girls' room. No girls in boys' room."

"I know that."

"Just reminding you."

Glin went back to his room.

Fran stepped inside. "All right, ladies. This isn't quite what we were expecting. I'm sure we're all disappointed, but let's make the best of it. After all, Logan is right, we're only here to sleep. For most of our stay, we're going to be unconscious."

"We'd have to be to survive it," Jay commented glumly.

"We'll be fine," Luci replied.

Fran nodded and left, closing the door behind her.

"This is terrible," Jay said.

"It's not so bad. It's clean."

"How can you tell?"

"You can smell the disinfectant."

"I'm gonna pass out with the stench of it." Jay crossed to the window and tried to open it. It wouldn't budge. She couldn't find the latch. "It's painted shut."

"Breathe shallow."

"Thank you."

"We're in a castle."

"We could be in the supply closet of a White Castle!"

"We're in Ireland. Did you ever in your wildest dreams think you'd be here?"

"What? In the tackiest room in all of Ireland? No. I never dreamed that."

"Are you okay?"

Jay didn't say anything for a long moment. "I'm really disappointed, Luci. I'm not good enough to be able to stay in a real castle, so I get to stay in a Sears castle."

"Of course you're good enough for a castle."

"Do you think Sam would wind up in a place like this? No, he'd be staying in the three-hundred-dollar a-night place."

Sam was a boy Jay had been in love with in Montreal. He was the heir to a very large shipping fortune, and because of Jay's racially mixed heritage, his parents didn't approve of his relationship with her. When Jay moved to America, she had felt the separation would be good for both of them, but obviously it was harder in practice than in theory.

"Is that what's bothering you?" Luci asked. "That this somehow reminds you of Sam?"

Jay sat up abruptly and went to the bathroom. "Everything reminds me of him. This is the difference between us. Three hundred million dollars' worth of difference. Even the universe knows it."

Luci went to the bathroom and watched as Jay brushed her teeth. "Whoa. You're starting to sound like Aimee. The universe has nothing to do with this hotel room. You're not being graded. This is just something that happened."

"Random."

"Yeah. Stacey has a ton of money. Daria maybe even more, and they're stuck here, too."

"That's true."

Luci waved her hand, mimicking Tammy Faye Bakker. "I like nice things," she drawled. "I deserve them."

Jay patted her face with a towel. "Overreacting, huh?"

"Girlfriend, just a little."

Jay hugged her. "Sorry."

"No big deal. Let's just go to sleep and get this part over with. Maybe it'll be a funny story we can tell later."

"How much later?"

"Many, many years."

Jay laughed softly. "It'll take that long."

A few minutes later they were both in bed.

"Have you heard from Sam recently?" Luci knew how much Jay cared for the young man she had left back in Montreal.

"I got a card just before I left. He was in B.C."

"British Columbia?"

"Uh-huh. He has some relatives in Vancouver."

"So what'd he say?"

"Misses me. Stuff like that."

"Don't think about it. Think about the room instead."

"I could."

"Are you doing it then?"

"I'll try. Where do you think they got this furniture?"

"A Russian garage sale."

"What?"

"Sure. Only that communists had taste this bad."
Jay laughed.

And at that moment the piano in the lounge on the first floor began to play.

"Luci . . ."

The singing began. Hearty voices joining in. Rousing, fun-loving voices loudly singing along to the pounding piano.

Jay pulled the pillow over her head.

"This can only go on for a while. Twenty minutes. Then they'll get tired and go home." Luci believed what she said.

An hour later the singing hadn't stopped.

"They have to be tired. It's almost midnight now. They'll be done soon. They've sung every song Neil Diamond ever did." Luci was trying hard to believe it.

Then they switched to Billy Joel.

An hour later the singing was still going strong.

"It's almost one . . ." Luci started.

"Do you know where your *voice* is?" Jay finished. "Luci, I'm so tired. I'm lying in a ditch with boards poking in my back and a honky-tonk downstairs."

Downstairs, the chorus had switched from Billy Joel to John Denver.

"I know."

There was a knock on the door.

"Who can that be?" Luci asked as she got out of bed.

"Maybe it's the Piano Man asking us to join in."

Luci opened the door to Stacey and Daria. "Come on in," she said.

Stacey and Daria entered and sat on the bed.

They all looked at each other.

"This is a nightmare," Stacey said.

"Would that I were so lucky to be asleep and only dreaming this," Jay commented.

"I'll go down and tell them to shut up," Stacey said.

"They have to stop soon. We can wait them out," Luci replied.

"Is anyone hungry?" Daria asked.

Jay nodded.

"I have some Chipsie Doodles," Daria offered.

"Okay. Let's have a party."

"Might as well."

Daria rushed out of the room.

"One more John Denver song and I'm going to scream," Jay said.

"Why aren't they singing Irish songs?" Luci asked.

"Because America has been so successful in exporting its entertainment," Stacey replied.

Daria reentered the room with a bag of snacks.

The music stopped.

The girls froze.

"Do you think . . ." Jay started.

"Don't jinx it!"

They held their breath.

The piano began thumping out "Take Me Home, Country Roads."

They all screamed.

At two o'clock the bar closed. They heard people leaving, the front door opening and closing, opening and closing. Cars drove away, spinning gravel with their tires.

"Well, that's a night," Luci said.

"See you tomorrow."

Luci closed the door and got back into bed. "We'll get a couple hours' sleep."

"I need it."

Luci switched off the light. "Good night, Jay."

"Good night, Luci."

Luci burrowed into her pillow. All she wanted was sleep.

It was then she heard the snoring.

"Jay?"

"Luci!" Jay wailed.

"Who is that?"

"It must be the man in the next room. These walls are so thin they're practically made of fiberboard."

"I can't sleep through that racket."

"Go rap on the wall; maybe it'll make him roll over or something."

"How do you know so much about it?" Luci asked.

"That's what they always do in the movies, isn't it?"

"Yes."

"I'm not getting out of bed again."

"Then we suffer." Luci switched on the light and glanced around. There was a phone book on the nightstand. She picked it up and hurled it at the wall.

There was a snort from the next room, then silence.

Jay and Luci raised thumbs to each other, rolled over, and went to sleep.

*   *   *

By seven, Luci and Jay were dressed and ready to leave. They left the room and there was complete silence.

"It should have been so quiet last night," Jay commented.

"Doesn't it seem odd? Shouldn't there be some life?"

"Like room service?" Jay teased.

Right then, Glin and Logan walked down the hall together.

"What about that singing last night?" Jay asked.

"What singing?" Logan looked perplexed.

"In the bar. The piano. The *singing*."

Glin shook his head. "We didn't hear anything. Fran moved us into another wing. Our room was way at the end of the hall and down another one."

"Figures."

"It was really ugly, though," Glin assured her.

Luci nodded.

They went down the beautiful staircase. The bottom floor was deserted. There wasn't a concierge, a waiter, or anyone else anywhere to be seen.

"What's going on?" Jay asked. "Isn't someone going to make us breakfast?"

There was a tap on the door.

They all looked at each other.

There was another tap on the door.

Logan walked over, unlocked the door, and opened it. The concierge was waiting outside.

"Thank you." He came inside. "How are you this morning?"

"We were locked in alone last night?" Luci asked in amazement.

"Yes, miss."

Luci stared at him. "There was no staff here to help us if something happened?"

"No, we close at two and my shift starts at seven."

"Who's supposed to let you in?"

"Someone always does."

Luci felt like bolting up the stairs, grabbing her things, grabbing Fran and dragging her to the van, and demanding to be driven anywhere. Immediately.

"What about breakfast?" Jay asked.

"We have a selection of cold cereal. Make yourselves comfortable in that room and I'll be right with you."

The concierge departed in the direction of the kitchen.

"Cold cereal?"

"It does seem a little meager."

"We have to get out of here! It's like being in a segment of the *Twilight Zone*," Luci moaned.

They raced up the stairs.

"The armory?" Logan asked as he got into the van.

"What about it?" Stacey replied.

"I wanted to see it."

"You're outvoted," Jay said.

Glin pushed the last of the luggage into the storage area, got in, and shut the door.

"Drive, Fran. Start the van and get us out of here," Luci begged.

Fran shook her head as she turned the key in the ignition. "Next stop?"

"Breakfast!" they replied in unison as Ballina Castle was put behind them.

Chapter Fourteen

"It can't be."

"It is."

"No."

"Yes."

They were standing on top of the cairn at Knocknarea. From that vantage point, they could see to the horizon, a vibrant green and beautiful Ireland spread around them on all sides. Finally, the sun was shining, brilliantly, warmly.

"This is man-made?"

"One thousand ninety-six feet worth," Fran confirmed.

"And who's supposed to be under here?" Stacey asked.

"Queen Maeve," Glin replied.

"Why would you bury someone under forty thousand tons of rock?"

"That's what you did in the Stone Age," Fran explained. "The greater the individual, the more pomp and circumstance went into the burial. Think of the pyramids of Egypt. All they are is a cairn in a different shape."

Luci tried to imagine people moving rocks and putting them in a mound that grew and grew until it was as big as a skyscraper. "If they ever excavate here, there are rocks under all this grass and dirt?"

"Yes. There's a famous passage grave in New-grange on the other side of Ireland that's been exca-vated and you can walk inside. There's a narrow path which leads into a rather large chamber. I suspect that's what's here, too."

"Why don't they find out?"

"These are all over Ireland. This is just the most impressive and the best preserved probably in all of Western Europe. Why disturb it?"

Luci shook her head in wonderment.

"Maybe there's a treasure," Logan said.

"Stop right there!" Jay ordered.

"There was treasure in all the pyramids," he reasoned.

Fran grinned. "We'll get a shovel in Knocknarea and you can start digging. Let's see . . . we'll come back for you in about a hundred years to see how things are going."

They began to retrace their path down the hill.

"We're not going to stop at every pile of rocks along the way, are we?" Stacey asked.

"Just the most intriguing ones," Fran answered.

Aimee pulled off her earphones. "These are sacred sites. They may even be energy centers, or have been placed on ley lines. A great deal of emotion has been invested in cairns; it's not surprising some people would feel a magnetic attraction to them."

"I'm not that interested in dead people," Daria admitted.

"They're not interested in you, either," Logan commented.

"Except the River House ghost," Jay remarked.

Daria grimaced.

Glin read the epitaph on the headstone.

"So who's the dead guy here?" Daria asked.

"William Butler Yeats," Luci said.

Daria didn't respond.

"A famous poet," Jay added. "He wrote those words."

"A spiritualist as well," Aimee continued. "The artists of the late nineteenth and early twentieth centuries were fascinated by metaphysics."

"What's that?" Daria asked.

Aimee smiled. "They were seeking answers to questions about life and death, reincarnation. Conan Doyle, Mark Twain, all explored the occult world."

Daria shrugged.

Aimee put her hand on the headstone and was lost in her own thoughts. Or perhaps those of someone else.

Glin stepped closer to Luci and whispered a poem in her ear.

"That's beautiful," Luci said.

"That's Yeats."

Fran refused to be put off by Daria's lack of enthusiasm. "Yeats died in 1939 but was buried in

France with the understanding he would be brought here at a later date. Which he was. Saint Colmcille began a monastery on this same site thirteen hundred years ago. All that remains is what's left of that round tower." Fran pointed. "And a high cross. Who wants to walk over there for a closer look? Hmm. Just about the reaction I was expecting."

North of Drumcliff they passed a large flat-topped hill.

"We're not stopping there, are we?" Stacey asked.

"Not if you don't want to," Fran answered.

"I'm not climbing up another cairn."

"That's not a passage grave, it's a mountain. Do you want to tell us what happened here at Benbulben, Glin?"

"Tain bo Cuailgne. The cattle raid of Cooley, one of the most famous of all Irish legends. Queen Maeve was a strong and powerful woman, a kingmaker. She had three requirements of her husbands — that they be generous, have no fear, and have no jealousy. She did have an eye for the men of her day, so perhaps that's why jealousy wasn't allowed in her husbands."

"Good for her," Jay applauded.

Glin smiled. "Maeve wanted the special bull of Cooley so she'd have wealth equal to that of her current husband. The hero Cúchulainn stood in the way of her plans. They were evenly matched opponents and the fight lasted quite awhile until

Maeve employed magic and managed to have him killed."

"Uh-huh." Daria was only impressed with legends involving horses.

Glin continued. "And it was here that Diarmaid fought the great boar of Beann Ghulban. When the boar charged, Diarmaid leaped on his back and after a terrible struggle was thrown off. He bled to death because Finn mac Cool wouldn't bring Diarmaid water, even though water from Finn's hands would heal any wound."

"Do none of these stories have a happy ending? You told us about the lovers that fell off the cliff. Now it's spurting blood. Before it was everyone hacking themselves to pieces. Didn't anyone ever get along?" Jay asked.

Fran shook her head. "I don't seem to recall that."

"Yeah," Jay grumbled. "Once we lost the matriarchal societies, peace was a dead issue."

Luci nodded. "That about sums it up."

"I think I should protest," Glin said.

Jay held back a grin. "It would be expected."

Glin thought about continuing but decided against it.

Fran put her arm around him. "A wise decision."

Logan shook his head. "Attack is the wise decision. Even when you're in retreat you attack."

Glin laughed. "Picture Logan running in one direction and shooting a bow and arrow in the opposite."

Luci smiled. "Piece of cake."

Fran opened her map. "I have some bad news for all you happy, happy travelers."

"What now?" Stacey groaned.

"No more sightseeing until Donegal or we won't make it to the cottage by dark."

"Seriously? No more schlepping?" Stacey asked.

"None."

"Fabulous," Stacey said, and everyone grinned.

"Donegal gets its name from the Vikings, who had a fort here in the nineteenth century. Dun na nGall means fort of the foreigners. For hundreds of years the county was controlled by the O'Donnell family . . ."

They were driving up a small hill toward the city.

"Fran!" Luci cried out. "A Quinnsworth! Please, stop."

"What's a Quinnsworth?" Daria asked.

"Another darn supermarket," Stacey replied.

"We do need supplies," Jay offered.

Fran turned into the parking lot. "Okay, we'll go to the supermarket." She shut off the engine. "But we're making this a fast trip. You're not going to pick up every single item and study it, right, Luci?"

"Oh, I promise," Luci said, hopping out of the van.

Twenty minutes later they were carrying sacks of groceries back to the van.

"I thought you were only staying for two nights," Stacey commented. "This is enough for a week."

"Only the way you eat," Daria said.

Stacey pulled herself up tall. "Meaning?"

"You eat like a bird," Daria said. "Don't you get hungry?"

Daria was always hungry.

"No."

"Well, I'm hungry now."

Fran sighed. "Should we find a place in Donegal?"

"It has been a while since breakfast," Jay admitted.

"At the center of town, there are restaurants and hotels. We can eat, see Donegal Castle, and be on our way."

The van headed back up the road and soon they were in the town where the Diamond Obelisk was visible.

Fran found a parking space nearby and they all got out. "In 1471, Hugh O'Donnell—yes, that O'Donnell family—and his wife, founded a Franciscan monastery."

Stacey groaned.

"Not to worry, Miss Rush," Fran continued. "It was blown up in 1601."

"Phew."

"Four of the monastery's friars chronicled the entire history of Ireland from the earliest known records to 1636. They knew the arrival of the English in Ireland meant the end of Celtic culture."

"How sad," Luci said.

"But we have a wealth of Celtic mythology thanks to them," Glin pointed out.

"The obelisk commemorates those four friars," Fran said as they walked closer. "There's a café across from the castle. It's about a block, Stacey. Does that sound acceptable?"

Everyone agreed to that and they began to walk through the main shopping district, pausing to look in the department-store windows as well as shops that catered to tourists. There were Aran sweaters by the boatload as well as feathery-light woolen cloth, throws, and scarves.

The café was pleasant and they ate a quick meal before crossing the street to the castle.

On the River Eske, the castle was the chief seat of the O'Donnell family, princes of Tir Chonaill.

"It doesn't have a roof," Stacey noted, looking up.

"It doesn't really have an inside, either," Daria said as they walked through the main entrance.

"There are walls," Glin pointed out.

"And beautiful ones they are," Luci said.

Jay looked up at the sky. Dark clouds were forming against the bright blue. "The weather's changing."

"One day of sun in a row is too much to hope for," Stacey grumbled.

Fran gathered them around her. "We can go to Glencolumbkille or we can go on to the cottage."

"What about Finn Lunny?" Luci asked. "How are we going to find him?"

"We could devote tomorrow to that project," Fran said.

Jay shook her head. "Someone said he was in Donegal and we're here now, so let's track him down."

"Maybe they meant the county of Donegal," Fran offered.

"There's a difference?" Daria asked.

Stacey rolled her eyes. "Yes."

"Then we have to do what we can," Logan said. "We should split up and hit every pub in town. Stacey, Daria, and Aimee go west. Glin and Luci go east. Jay and I will go north. And Fran can stay at the van."

Everyone agreed, except Fran. "Excuse me, Logan, but do you seriously think I would consider letting you all go off on your own?"

"Sure."

"No way. We'll all stay together. That way none of us can get into trouble." Fran sent Logan a meaningful glance.

"Wasting time and manpower," Logan shrugged.

"Uh-huh."

Three hours later they were in a café having tea and knowing only that the elusive Finn Lunny did not live in Donegal town. No one knew where he did live. Someone said Letterkenny. Someone else said the Bloody Foreland. Or that Finn had lived on Aran Island for a time but now lived in Dublin because that was where the recording industry was.

Everyone had a different version of Finn Lunny's recent history. He had worked with the Hothouse Flowers. Produced for U2. Appeared in an Enya video. Toured with Simple Pleasures. He was in Australia walking his song line. Was in New York. Nepal. London. He had married. Had a broken heart. Was living a monastic life on the Skellig Islands.

Glin shook his head. "This man is all over the map."

"We need to find his parents," Logan said. "They probably have a house, unless they're nomads, too. That means they have an address. We find them and we find the son. Simple."

"Someone mentioned the father's name."

"Leo."

"Right. They said he had a pub, that everyone knows him."

Glin drained his cup. "We'll retrace our steps and ask about the father."

Fran raised her hand. "Hold on. Time's running out for today. If we don't leave for the cottage now, we're going to get there very late."

"I can stay up late," Logan assured her.

"I know that. We'll be driving out in the country, in the dark, and by the look of the sky, in some bad weather. Our only choice is to head north and start the search tomorrow. Okay?"

With that decided, they headed back to the van.

"I hope it's worth tracking him down," Stacey commented.

Glin said nothing.

"What else do we have to do?" Jay asked.

"I had a call in to CNN International," Stacey replied. "We can have international condemnation of the Blazers with two minutes of video run at the top of the hour."

"We can have both," Luci stated. "Finn and CNN."

"You can never have everything," Aimee said.

"This isn't everything, it's just two things," Jay replied.

Chapter Fifteen

The sky grew darker and the wind speed picked up the farther north they went. The landscape grew progressively more dramatic—rocky and bleak but also beautiful and compelling. Fran had turned on the radio hoping to get some traditional Irish music, but it seemed that there was only pop from America.

"Two radio stations. Two television stations," Stacey commented. "Nothing on but talking heads discussing the pros and cons of road construction."

"Don't forget *Dynasty*."

Stacey grimaced. "Like I said. Nothing on."

"There's nothing on in America even if you have cable," Luci pointed out. "Thirty-six channels. All running repeats of *Murder, She Wrote*."

"We don't have cable in the valley; it's too remote. We have a satellite dish," Daria said.

"What's that like?" Jay asked.

"You get everything. See, there are a whole bunch of satellites in the sky. You can move the dish to any of them and pick up what they're beaming. We get Mexico and Canada. Dubai TV. Japan."

"So what's on?" Logan asked.

"Not much. We play TV games," Daria explained.

"Like *Jeopardy* or *Wheel of Fortune*?" Luci asked.

Daria shook her head. "No. We made up these games. I have a friend who lives on the other side of the valley. We set a time limit of thirty minutes and the goal is to try to find the same actor on different channels at the same time."

Luci struggled with this concept. "I don't get it."

"You'd try to find like William Shatner in *Star Trek, T.J. Hooker,* and *Rescue 911*. Plus there are television movies he was in. The one with the spiders or was it fire ants? There are probably a hundred channels to search through, so you have to be fast."

Jay rolled her eyes.

"Or you can do it by the day. How many times can you find Lindsay Wagner. The first place you look is Lifetime TV. She's made a ton of TV movies."

"And this is how you spend your day?" Logan asked.

"If I'm not riding, I'm not really allowed off the ranch. Except to go to school."

No one said anything for a long moment.

Jay leaned over. "Do you watch a lot of television, Stacey?"

"My father's show. *All Our Days.* My best friend,

Ariel, has a role, so I want to watch her, but I don't have time for all the rest."

Luci couldn't imagine having nothing to do but watch television. Of course, her parents hadn't imprisoned her in the apartment, either.

"We have a television, but it could be broken," Glin said.

"Don't you know?" Daria asked.

Glin shrugged. "I don't think anyone has turned it on in a couple years."

"Is there a television at this cottage?" Daria asked.

"I doubt it," Fran replied.

Daria grimaced. "What will we do all evening?"

"We can play charades," Stacey said. "Not."

For a moment Luci had been worried. She couldn't picture them standing up and acting out clues. Actually, the scary part was that she could imagine it all too clearly and it was the activity Luci wanted to do least in her entire life.

"It might have been fun," Aimee offered.

Logan stared at her.

"We'll find something to do, I'm sure," Fran added.

As the day grew darker and the sky more ominous, they arrived in Dungloe, a small city near the ocean. Stores and businesses lined the narrow streets, and since it was the end of the business day, people were hurrying home.

"We have a choice to make right now," Fran began. "We can stop here for dinner or we can go to the cottage."

"How much farther is the cottage?" Daria asked.

"Since I've never been there before, I'm guessing an hour. If we don't eat now, we'll have a late dinner."

Daria shook her head.

"I can't stand hearing about hunger pangs every five minutes," Stacey declared. "Let's eat and get it over with."

"It should be more fun than that," Luci suggested.

"Why?"

"Because we're all together. It's a celebration," Glin explained.

Stacey shrugged. "The longer you sit at the table, the more you eat. It's defeating the purpose, isn't it?"

"Just don't eat more than you want," Jay suggested.

"Then what do you do?"

"Talk," Glin answered.

"In Montreal you go to a restaurant and stay for hours," Jay explained. "It's not like eating fast food. You're not having a race to see who can finish first."

"Doesn't your family get together for meals and tell each other what happened during the day?" Luci asked.

"Be serious. My father's at the studio until midnight almost every day," Stacey replied.

The McKennitts had dinner together every night unless Luci's mother had a special affair to cater. It was a time Luci looked forward to, and she couldn't envision eating alone in her room or an empty apartment. It was no wonder Stacey never enjoyed her food. She was eating under the worst conditions conceivable.

Fran parked the van in front of Maloney's Hotel. "Everyone out. We'll eat here."

"There may be someplace else . . ." Luci started thumbing through her guidebook.

"There may be, but we're not driving around to find out."

Standing on the sidewalk, they could feel the change in the weather. It was quite cool and damp and the wind was blowing with some authority.

They began to walk up the steps to the hotel.

"If where we're staying is a thatched cottage, will the roof leak during a rain?" Daria asked.

Fran opened the door to the hotel. "No. Even a real thatched roof is waterproof. Most thatched roofs now have tin underneath for protection and to preserve all the work."

"It's a dying art, isn't it?" Glin commented.

"Afraid so," Fran replied as they entered the dining room and found a large table near the window. "I've seen cottages where the thatch was woven into designs. Not many people can do that anymore."

A ruddy-faced woman approached with menus. "Good evening. Will you be having our special tonight?"

Fran nodded.

"What is it?" Luci asked. She wasn't likely to agree to dinner without knowing what it was.

"Baked ham, potatoes, salad, and soup. Bread. Dessert."

Logan grinned. "Outstanding."

Stacey sighed. "Fine. What's the difference."

"Lovely," the woman replied as she wrote the order down on her pad.

"Miss," Glin began. "Do you know the Lunny family?"

"Are they supposed to live in Dungloe? I've never heard of them."

"The county. Leo Lunny has a pub someplace. His son is a musician."

The woman pondered this for a time, then shook her head. "I'm sorry. I can't help you." She turned and went toward the kitchen.

"We'll find him," Logan said.

"Where's a listing of all the pubs in the county?" Jay asked.

Fran put her napkin on her lap. "The tourist office might have something like that. Letterkenny is a big enough town to have one of those; and that's fairly close. There's Glenveagh National Park on the way."

"What's there?"

"Gardens. A castle."

"Walking," Stacey interjected.

Soon the multicourse meal began arriving, and within minutes the entire table was covered with serving dishes mounded with food.

"Two kinds of potatoes?" Stacey asked, recoiling.

Logan dipped his spoon into one bowl. "Yeah, isn't it great?"

Each dinner plate had several layers of ham and gravy, potatoes, and green beans. There was a large basket of bread, both white and soda, and a dish of butter.

After they ate their way through all this, the table was cleared and then dessert arrived. It was a dish of fresh kiwis smothered in clotted cream.

Stacey attempted to scrape the heavy cream off as the others relished their dessert. "Have they never heard of a low-fat diet?"

"I guess not," Logan replied, spooning up the cream from Stacey's bread plate.

As they were working their way to the bottom of the dishes, a young man wearing an apron tied around his waist came out of the kitchen.

"Marie said you were looking for a musician."

"We are," Glin admitted. "Finn Lunny."

"Ah, Finn. He's a hard one to find, but his father isn't. Leo has a pub in Gweedore. Go there and ask him. He may know where his son is. I've been to the pub and seen Finn play. He's a great musician. If you find Finn, tell him we want to see him again."

"I will," Glin replied.

Logan finished dessert. "We find Gweedore to-morrow and the next day we get an early start back to River House. That way we won't miss the hunt."

"Let's not talk about the hunt," Fran suggested.

Logan was confused. "Why not?"

"Because some of us don't think it's a very good idea," Jay explained.

"That's your opinion. You're welcome to it," Logan said. "But it's not my opinion."

"I don't think hunting—" Jay began.

"You think that," Logan interrupted. "Other people don't agree. Once you artificially remove the natural predators from an environment, unwanted animals will thrive. How are you going to keep that population contained?"

"Unwanted animals?" Luci asked.

"You take wolves out of the equation and suddenly you are overrun with foxes," Logan replied calmly. "There's one solution."

Luci stood. "I'll see you guys outside." She left the table.

Jay glared at Logan as Glin went after Luci.

"What did I do?" Logan asked.

"You're so dense."

"I am?"

"You're insensitive!" Jay replied.

"No. I'm practical. I understand the necessity for wildlife management."

Jay dropped her napkin on the table. "This upsets Luci. It bothers me. If you were sensitive to our feelings, you wouldn't talk about this in front of us. Get it?"

Logan looked from Jay to Fran.

Fran nodded.

"Oh," Logan said.

Luci was waiting by the van as Glin arrived.

"What do you want to do about this?"

"I don't want to go on the hunt. I'll just stay in my room."

"Okay," Glin said as he leaned up against the van.

"You can go if you want to."

"I don't want to. It was just something to do. I don't hunt in Vermont."

Luci looked at him.

"Well, actually, we have. If I came back with a very nice pheasant, are you telling me you wouldn't want to cook that bird up in a spectacular way?"

Luci closed her eyes. "I don't know what the answer is."

"When you get all your food under plastic at the supermarket, it's a different thing than going after it yourself."

"Exactly! If this was about feeding people, I could understand it a little better. If the odds were more equal, it would seem more humane. This is unfair . . . it's sport. It's about people having fun at the expense of an animal."

"I agree."

"You probably think I'm naive. Or out of touch with the real world. Jungle rules."

"No, I agree with you."

"You probably think—"

Glin put his hand over her mouth. "I agree with you."

"Really?"

"Yes."

"People use animals in all kinds of ways. This one needs to be rethought."

"I wish we could have done something. . . ."

"If you still feel that way when you get home, we'll figure out something together."

"You'd do that?"

Glin nodded.

"I'd like that."

Chapter Sixteen

There wasn't a light anywhere on the island.

They had left the mainland and crossed over a causeway onto Cruit Island. The narrow paved road turned into an even narrower dirt track, which wound around and around until finally a white cottage appeared in the headlights.

"Here we are," Fran said as she read the small sign on the side of the building. Cruit Cottage.

"It's cute," Jay exclaimed as she opened the van door.

The cottage was plain. There were no shutters on the windows, no bushes or plants near the foundation, no trees. But there was a thatched roof made of brown reeds.

Luci stepped out of the van and instantly the wind ripped her small plastic bag out of her hands. It was like being in a wind tunnel.

Jay leaned into the wind. "Umm. Something something something!"

"What?" Luci said.

Jay repeated her sentence. All the words were lost to the Atlantic.

"What?"

"I can't walk!" Jay shouted.

Daria's nylon jacket blew off.

Stacey gripped the door handle.

"This is a hurricane!" Luci shouted.

"Isn't Mother Nature wonderful?" Aimee beamed.

Logan pressed his body against the wind. "This must be over sixty knots! Grab on!" He held out his hand to Jay.

They formed a line, holding hands, and struggled to the front door, leaning at an impossible angle all the way.

Luci's eyes were filled with wind-whipped tears as she scooted inside the cottage and Fran shut the door.

The wind howled outside.

"When did that happen? It was okay in Dungloe."

"You don't know what it's like on this side of the Atlantic," Fran said. "I spent time on the islands and this kind of weather is normal."

"How can people live like this?" Stacey asked. "You'd never walk standing straight up."

"Oh, they do." Fran smiled. "Once in a while."

Luci stepped into the spacious living room. The furniture was plain and functional, made of light pine with colorful cushions on the chairs and sofa. Bright lamps were positioned on the end tables. At one end of the room there was a small fireplace with a brass bucket full of peat bricks.

"Could we have a fire?" Luci asked.

"That's what it's there for," Fran replied. "Knock yourself out."

Luci crouched by the hearth and began arranging some kindling and paper as the guys made a second trip to the van to get the rest of the groceries.

"Is this a traditional cottage?" Jay asked.

Fran glanced around. There was a small galley kitchen, a utility room, two bedrooms downstairs, and a large loft. "Yes. Except in the past, the animals would be living right about there." She pointed to one end of the living room.

"No one would be that stupid," Daria said.

"It wasn't stupid at all. Animals generate a lot of heat. Hundreds of years ago, before nice fireplaces like that, all there was was a hole in the roof for the smoke to go out. People needed all the heat they could get. Most of them didn't have enough money or resources to construct a separate building for the animals. It was practical for them all to live together under one roof."

"And smelly," Stacey commented.

"Bathing was not a priority," Fran admitted.

The door banged open as Logan and Glin entered. They both leaned against the wooden door to close it. "Last time out tonight," Logan decreed.

"And it's starting to rain," Glin added.

Luci held a match to the paper, then blew on the small flame to encourage it to spread to the kindling. "It'll be so cozy in here with a fire and the rain outside."

Daria flopped on the sofa. "There's nothing to do."

"Don't you have something to read?" Jay asked. "No."

"Here's a game." Logan pointed to the wall. "It's a target thing. You throw these Ping-Pong balls covered in Velcro. Darts but round." He pulled several balls off the target, took several steps back, and tossed them at the bull's-eye.

"Oh, that's fun," Stacey remarked as Logan hit the bull's-eye three times in a row.

"We could do it with our opposite hand," Glin suggested as Logan took aim again.

"That's a challenge," Jay said as Logan hit the bull's-eye three more times.

"I'm sorry. You can't blame me if I'm ambidextrous."

"Naturally or did you cultivate it?" Luci asked. She could imagine Logan spending hours training his left hand to be as facile as his right.

"Born that way, Miss Luci," Logan replied.

"Let's get the groceries put away and then we can talk about what else is possible."

"I've got a surprise," Luci said as she left the fire in the hearth.

"Umm?" Stacey sat in a chair and folded her arms in front of her.

"It'll take me twenty minutes. Jay, you want to help?" Luci went into the kitchen.

"Lead the way, Julia Child."

"Close the door. I don't want anyone sneaking a peek."

"Can you give us a hint?"

"No."

"I'll bet it's fattening," Stacey commented.

"Is not," Luci replied, and Jay closed the door.

Luci began to rummage through the bags of groceries and pulled out a box of sugar, some Spanish peanuts, and a container of popcorn.

"What are you going to make?"

"You'll see. I need a large saucepan. Two of them. Put some oil in them. Enough to cover the bottom. And we'll need lids."

Jay bent down and began going through the well-stocked cabinets, pulling out pots and lids. She put them on the burners, poured a few tablespoons of oil into each pot, and then waited as the oil grew hot.

Luci put popcorn kernels into each pot and then covered them with lids. "Now we need a couple big bowls."

"We're having popcorn and what else?"

Luci grinned as she poured a teacup full of sugar into a small pan then added some water. "My favorite."

In a moment there was a pop followed by several more.

"Shake those pans," Luci instructed.

Jay began to move the pans back and forth over the burners. Luci melted the sugar and butter and stirred it as it began to grow hotter.

"I never thought I'd be in a cottage in Ireland making . . . Come on, Luce, fill in the blank."

"You'll see."

"This cottage is so much nicer than Ballina Castle."

"That was grim." Luci laughed. "Funny, though."

Jay looked out the kitchen window into the blackness. Rain pelted the window. "One day we stay in a castle, the next a thatched cottage. We're so lucky."

Luci nodded. "We really did win the lottery in France."

"Before that. When we signed up for that trip, I'd say. Otherwise how would we have met?"

"That's true. I can't imagine better friends."

"What about Logan? Sometimes I want to strangle him."

Luci dripped sugar mixture into a glass of water. It formed a ball as it cooled. "Wouldn't you miss him if he wasn't here?"

"Maybe."

"I would."

Luci removed the sugar from the heat and stirred it.

The popcorn finished popping and Jay poured it into two large bowls. "Now what?"

"Oil your hands," Luci said as she held out the bottle.

Jay made a face as the oil dripped onto her palms.

Luci drizzled the sugar syrup onto the popcorn, threw in several handfuls of peanuts, and grabbed a handful. "Compress it into balls. And work fast," Luci said as she finished her first popcorn ball.

Soon they had formed all the popcorn into balls and put them back in the bowls.

"It's like Cracker Jacks."

"It's actually more like Crunch 'n Munch," Luci admitted. "I spent weeks trying to figure out their recipe, but I finally did it." Pushing open the door, she went out into the living room and walked over to Stacey, offering her the first popcorn ball.

Stacey appeared unsure, then took one. "Thank you."

Luci held out the bowl. "Don't be shy."

In a flash, everyone had one and was enthusiastically biting into it.

"These are outstanding." Logan reached for his second.

"Wonderful!"

"You did this from scratch?" Daria asked.

Luci took one and sat on the sofa near Glin. "Of course. I never make anything from a box."

"I didn't know you could make these at home," Daria admitted.

"A hundred years ago there *were* no boxes," Fran commented.

Daria took a huge bite, finishing the popcorn ball. "What did people do?"

Luci held back a smile.

Stacey wiped her fingers on a tissue. "They managed."

By ten o'clock Luci and Jay were in bed, anxious to get a good night's sleep after being serenaded into the wee hours of the morning at Ballina Castle.

Luci's mattress was so soft it virtually didn't have insides to it. "How's your bed?"

"Sleep to the side," Jay offered. "It's better than the middle."

Luci moved over. Jay was right. She couldn't feel the slats underneath the mattress anymore. "Better. Good night."

"Night."

Luci snuggled into the covers. She could hear the rain on the windows and smell the peat smoke. It was very pleasant and she began to drift off to sleep.

There was a knock on the door.

"Please . . ." Luci murmured.

The knock was repeated.

"Who's there?" Jay asked, annoyance permeating her voice.

"Stacey. May I come in?"

Luci switched on the light and looked to Jay in amazement. Jay raised her hands in bewilderment.

"Sure. Come on."

Stacey opened the door and entered as Luci sat up in the bed. Her butt hit the slats.

"I've been thinking about the hunt," Stacey began.

"Now?" Jay asked.

"Yes."

"Can't it wait till morning?"

"I think I have a solution. If you want to wait till morning . . ."

Luci shook her head. "No. Tell us."

"Somebody needs to go to the master of foxhounds and someone else has to talk to Ethne. We have to convince them to cooperate."

Jay lay back down. "They were in love thirty years ago. That's over. They hate each other now."

"It does seem like a long shot," Luci admitted.

"If they were in love once, there must be something left," Stacey insisted. "At least enough to get them to find a neutral ground."

"In Switzerland, maybe, but not in Ireland. Their beliefs are completely in opposition to each other. They've been fighting about this for years. What are we going to say that will change their minds?"

"I think I have that figured out, too."

Jay sat up. "I'm all ears."

First thing the next morning Luci woke, dressed silently, and went outside. The wind had died down, the rain had stopped, and the sun was almost visible behind the thin clouds on the horizon. She went across the lawn and picked her way down the rocky hillside to the ocean. The breeze smelled salty and blew her hair back as she walked along the shore. Mounds of kelp had washed up.

"Dulaman."

Luci looked up in surprise to see Glin standing nearby.

"The word for kelp is *dulaman* in Irish."

"What are you doing out here so early?"

"Being landlocked, I don't get much chance to

see the ocean. When I'm nearby, I like to take advantage of it."

"Are you having a good time here?"

Glin nodded. "Are you?"

"Yes. It's lovely. Even if it is a little damp."

"I think the Dublin side of the island is sunnier."

"Now you tell me!" Luci laughed.

"This was the tour we could all take."

"I don't regret it."

"Logan doesn't mean everything quite the way it sounds," Glin said suddenly.

"I know."

"We'll work on him."

They strolled along the sand, seagulls flying above the water. The sun was brighter, the clouds disappearing.

"Do you think Logan would help us if we had a solution to the conflict between Ethne and Brendan?"

Glin paused. "He'll say it's none of his business."

"It's none of my business."

Glin stopped him as he walked past. "Logan, why don't you hear her out."

"I'm not here to play Cupid," Logan insisted.

"No one said anything about that," Jay interjected. "We just want them to be able to speak civilly to each other."

"Get real. Did you see how he powered her out of the pub?" Logan shoved the rest of his clothes into his duffel bag and zipped it shut.

"It might work if you helped," Luci pointed out.

Logan shook his head and left the cottage.

Jay gritted her teeth. "He's so obstinate."

Chapter Seventeen

The road to Gweedore was narrow and the van was the only vehicle on it. They had traveled through the Bloody Foreland, named not for a battle but for the reddish tinge to the rocks at sunset. Since it was early afternoon, there was no rosy glow to the scenery. There were peat bogs, some with heavy machinery cutting into the earth.

"Listen to this," Jay said as she read the travel guide. "The peat bogs are being harvested so intensively that what took ten thousand years to create will be destroyed in a matter of a few more years."

"Figures," Stacey grumbled.

"All manner of artifacts have been found in bogs," Fran added. "It's a great preservative. Bodies from five thousand years ago still wearing their leather garments have been retrieved. Butter. Cheese."

"So there could be something very old hidden in one of those bogs."

"Count on it."

Gweedore was a very small town set on the hillsides. The modest buildings were plain and white, much like Cruit Cottage. The yards were neat with a few plants or shrubs for landscaping.

"Listen to this," Jay said as she read from the guide book. "At the turn of the century, Gweedore was a major manufacturing center for rugs in Arts and Crafts designs."

"Does it say if there's a police station?" Luci asked. "They'd know where the Lunnys lived."

"Doesn't mention that," Jay admitted.

"But it's a good suggestion. The police are called gardai here," Fran replied. "Keep your eyes peeled for one."

As they drove on, there was a farmer walking by the roadside and Fran stopped.

"Dia Dhuit," she said. *"Ba mhaith liom dul go dti Leo Lunny?"*

The man smiled broadly. "You're looking for Leo, are you? Straight up, take a left and follow that until you get to a dirt track. His place is there."

"Gur a mhile maith agat. Thank you."

"Ta failte romhat," he replied, and tipped his hat.

Fran headed the van up the road.

"They speak English without an accent. Well, they have an Irish accent, of course," Daria noted.

"English is probably their first language," Fran said. "There are a few schools in Donegal that are strictly Irish speaking now, but this is a fairly recent action taken by those who want to preserve their native language. Here the state language is English and the Irish are in the minority."

"In their own country!" Luci added.

Fran turned off the main road. "Irish is a difficult language. There are several dialects which can be quite different. Very confusing."

Soon the road narrowed and up ahead there was a white building on the left side.

"What do you think?"

"There's no sign outside."

"Must be it. It's not a house."

"Right." Fran pulled into the drive and parked the van.

Glin hopped out. "I'll check." In a half-dozen strides he was at the door and stepped inside.

"The quest for this Lunny guy has to end here," Stacey remarked. "We can't trail him all over the countryside. We don't have time."

"That's true. As long as we find the father, that should satisfy Glin," Jay said. "Shouldn't it?"

Luci nodded. "Isn't he taking a long time in there?"

"Maybe he got lost," Daria offered.

Luci got out of the van. "Let's see what's keeping him."

They walked to the building and entered. Inside, there were four musicians playing at one end of the dark pub. Glin stood near the doorway silently, watching.

The song ended and one of the men looked at them. "Can I help you?"

"Finn?" Glin said.

The young man grinned. "Guilty."

Glin walked to the stage and offered his hand.

"We've been all over Donegal looking for you. I'm Glin Woods."

Finn shook Glin's hand heartily then put down his guitar. "Why would you waste your holiday looking for me?"

The other men laughed.

"I wanted to say that the way you play the uillean pipes defies human ability."

The man on drums groaned. "Don't tell him that! His head will become so big, it will stretch from here to Londonderry!"

Finn gave them a look. "I'll be the one to decide when I've had enough compliments." He stepped off the stage. "They're a jealous lot. But they're my cousins, so I can't fire them."

An older man entered the pub from the back room.

"Da!" Finn called to him. "We have visitors from America! This is my father, Leo Lunny."

"*Cead mhile failte.* What can I get you?"

Stacey pulled her jacket around her. "Tea?"

"Lovely. Tea all around?"

They nodded and found a table.

"So what brings you here?" Finn asked.

"You," Luci replied.

"I didn't think you were serious," Finn replied.

"It *is* hard to believe," Stacey agreed, glancing around the dark room.

The pub was a long building and seemed to be without a heat source except for a fireplace at one end. There were a few ceiling light fixtures, but they weren't turned on, so it was quite dark. The floor was stone. All of which made the room quite cold and damp.

One of the cousins came down from the stage and began to make a peat fire in the hearth. "You probably don't find this cold to your liking, but it's normal for us."

Luci shoved her hands in her pockets and prayed the tea wouldn't cool off too much before it reached them. The hot cup would warm her hands.

"I was raised with traditional music. My father's a musician in a trio called Rosewood," Glin explained.

"Sometimes Glin fills in," Logan interjected.

"So we have a fellow musician. Lads!" Finn called out. "This one is one of us."

Glin shook his head. "Hardly."

"Go on with you." Finn stood and dragged Glin to his feet. "What do you play?"

"Keyboard. Guitar . . ."

"James, give the lad my guitar!" In one leap, Finn had jumped back onto the stage. "Let's make some music!"

Reluctantly, Glin slipped on the guitar strap.

Jay leaned over to Luci. "Is Glin going to be able to do this?"

"I don't have a clue," Luci whispered back. She would never be able to get up and perform in a million years. How could he play with four men he'd met only minutes ago?

Luci crossed her fingers for him.

"He'll be great," Logan told them. "Haven't you ever heard him play?"

Luci shook her head.

Logan turned his chair toward the stage. "Then you're in for a treat."

There was a brief conference between the members of the group, then they began. For the next twenty minutes they played rock and roll, old tunes and new, songs Luci recognized and some she did not, but all of them were wonderful. Soon everyone was on their feet, clapping and dancing along.

There was a pause for a moment while Finn picked up his pipes and stepped forward. "This is one of my favorites and Glin says it's one of his as well. Why a young American lad would know this old tune is beyond me but here it is. 'Chuaigh Me 'Na Rosann.'"

Unable to understand a word of Irish, Luci still felt everything being said. The music filled the room and enveloped her in its gentle rhythm. When Finn played the pipes, it seemed that a human voice had begun to sing of sorrow and strength, of defeat and triumph. It was like listening to music from another realm, a magical place where brave warriors would never grow old and where beautiful women could run as fast as horses.

The last notes of the song faded and no one moved.

Finn looked at the audience. "Dead, are you?"

Logan was the first to spring into action, jumping to his feet and applauding enthusiastically. The rest joined in.

"Didn't I tell you he was great?" Logan asked.

Luci nodded. This was the first time she had

thought of Glin as a musician and she didn't know quite what to make of it. Something changed.

Glin shook Finn's hand. Hearty thumps on the back were exchanged by the group and they all stepped off the stage.

"More tea?" Leo asked as everyone gathered around the table.

"Your best for our friends, Da," Finn replied. "If we treat them well, maybe this one will come back and play with us again." He pointed at Glin.

"Only if you come to America first," Glin replied.

"You don't know Finn." One of the cousins laughed. "He might just take you up on it!"

"I hope he does. My parents would be thrilled. We'd invite everyone in town."

Finn laughed. "What a party that would be!"

That was one party Luci wouldn't want to miss.

The mist turned into a heavy drizzle as they drove back to the cottage. Daria fell asleep with her head against the window while the others talked about what they would do that evening after dinner. It was decided that they'd go to an early movie in Bunbeg, a small city nearby. But once they arrived, they discovered the movie house was closed and the plans changed to having dinner at a restaurant across from the harbor then taking a walk along the water.

Large oceangoing vessels were at the docks, cargo being unloaded from the holds. It was a busy port with longshoremen hurrying about, forklifts being ridden from one end of the dock to the other, trucks entering and leaving, horns tooting, the foghorn wailing off the coast.

"Was Finn all you imagined?" Luci asked Glin as they strolled down the dock.

"And more," Glin admitted.

"I'm glad for you."

"At least it was something to take everyone's mind off Ethne and Brendan."

Luci nodded. "Even if Logan doesn't stick with us, I think we can make it work."

Jay came up behind them. "Make what work?"

"The animal-rights thing."

"Stacey still wants to contact CNN International."

They all paused where they were and Aimee stopped with a large shell in her hand.

"Someone used to live here," she said.

"Right," Jay replied.

Stacey approached. "Are we wet enough and cold enough now to go back to the cottage?"

Luci had to agree. She'd been cold most of the day and even her heavy sweater hadn't helped much.

"Let's call it a night," Jay said, and glanced around.

Fran was down at the end of the dock waving at the boat. "Logan, get off that gangplank right now! You have no business being on that ship!"

Logan stopped in midstride. "But I wanted to ask the captain about the marine forecast."

"On the dock—*now!*"

Logan began to walk back. "It would be very helpful if we had a decent weather report."

"He can't be serious," Jay said. "It's going to be cold—"

"And damp," Luci finished.

Thoughtfully, Stacey studied Glin's long waxed-cotton raincoat. She reached out and touched the dark green cloth. "I want one of these."

Luci was gripped by a moment of fear as she imagined the endless shopping quest they'd suffer through trying to find a raincoat that suited Stacey's high standards. Jay was already thumbing through the guidebook at top speed.

"Magee's of Donegal. Right on the way home."

"Thank you," Stacey said.

Jay closed the book with a sigh. "My pleasure."

Chapter Eighteen

"**W**e have to get coordinated," Stacey said as they entered the library at River House for afternoon tea.

Logan reached for the plate of sandwiches and took several then passed it along to Glin. "Why do you have to butt into something that's none of your business?"

Stacey ignored him. "I'm going to stay here and get on the phone. Who's going to town?"

Luci raised her hand. "I'll talk to Ethne."

"I'll go with you," Jay offered.

"Good. Glin, will you go to Brendan?" Stacey asked.

Logan leaned back in the wing chair. "Don't do it."

Stacey glared at Logan. "No one is asking you to do anything. This is about us. It's something we want to do."

Logan looked from Luci to Jay to Glin. "I can't

believe you would actually get involved with something so . . ."

"So what?" Jay asked.

"So dumb!" Logan exploded. "We're guests here. They're following their traditions. What's the prime directive? Don't involve yourself in another civilization."

"This is not *Star Trek*!" Stacey shot back. "This is Earth. Our prime directive is to nurture our home planet!"

"There is much to be said for having reverence for all of life," Aimee admitted.

Jay leaned toward Logan. "If you're so worried about the population of foxes exploding, there must be a scientific—"

"A humane," Luci added.

"—solution . . . like birth control," Jay finished.

Logan stared at her. "Birth control?"

Jay glared back at him. "I'm not suggesting it would be in the same form as human terms. But maybe veterinarians could capture some individuals and give them an implant. . . ."

"Or minor surgery," Daria offered. "Depending on the gender."

"I want you people to know that your blips have gone right off the radar screen," Logan said, standing up.

Stacey put down her teacup. "Thank you for pointing that out. It convinces me I'm doing the right thing."

"Even if you could convince all the members of

the hunt to go along with whatever scheme you've come up with, it's not going to make a difference," Logan replied.

"Big storms are heralded by a gentle breeze," Aimee remarked.

Luci gave Aimee a thumbs-up.

"That's right," Jay agreed.

Logan turned to Glin. "Do you agree with them?"

Glin nodded.

Logan shook his head in disgust and left the library.

"Okay. That issue is settled," Stacey said. "Now who is going to Brendan's? Glin?"

Luci and Jay found Ethne's cottage on the outside of town not far from River House. Unlike most cottages, this one was made of fieldstone, and dark green English ivy covered the chimney completely. They paused at the gate.

"Logan's right in a way," Luci said tentatively.

"Not this time."

"It's really not our business. It's a good idea but—"

"Don't tell me you want to back out now!"

"No, not that." Luci threw up her hands in resignation. "Go for it, girl." She marched to the front door and gave the brass knocker a sharp rap.

In a few moments Ethne came to the door. "My! What a surprise! Do come in."

Luci and Jay entered the house. It was warm and welcoming, with some dark antiques and a dark floor but brightened by floral fabrics and light walls.

"What brings you here?"

Luci took a breath. "We're not trying to solve your problem—"

"Yes, we are," Jay interjected.

"In a way."

Ethne sat down in an upholstered chair and motioned for them to join her.

Luci clasped her hands. "Our friend Stacey has done a bit of hunting and she thinks she has a solution."

Ethne smiled. "You're preaching to the converted. Brendan is the one who resists all attempts at negotiation."

"We have someone at his stable now," Jay said.

"Well, ladies, you seem to have thought this thing through. What's the solution?"

"They don't want to stop hunting. And it's really not fair that anyone should dictate someone else's activities."

"Yes . . ."

"The problem is coming up with an arrangement that doesn't offend your sensibilities and doesn't interfere with the hunt." Luci sounded very convincing and reasonable.

"That's impossible," Ethne replied.

"Maybe not," Jay said. "What if you could both have almost what you want?"

Ethne tilted her head slightly. "As I said, I'm willing to make compromises up to a point."

"You don't have any objection to riders knocking

themselves out running up and down the hills, right?"

"They can ride themselves so hard their seat-bones poke through the seat of their pants as far as I'm concerned."

"Just as long as no foxes are involved," Jay said.

"Or hares or badgers," Ethne added.

Luci nodded. "The hunt would be limited to horses and riders and those smelly dogs."

"They're called hounds. Never a dog." Ethne smiled. "If you remove the prey from the equation, you have a hack, and none of these people are interested in that."

"Hack?" Luci asked.

"Quiet ride," Jay explained.

"Right. All you'd have is a hack and that's not exciting. The fun part—although I can't understand it—and don't get me wrong, I haven't tried to comprehend any of this rushing-around business—is to chase after those . . . hounds, with all the commotion."

"And the mystery," Jay added. "You never know where you're going."

Ethne nodded. "I would say those are not negotiable aspects of the hunt."

"We have it covered," Jay assured her.

"Stacey says there's a thing called a drag," Luci said.

Ethne raised her eyebrows.

"On a drag hunt, someone ties a rope to a piece of meat and drags it over hill and dale," Jay continued.

Luci was growing more excited and confident. It made sense. "The scent is left on the ground. The hounds don't know the difference. They run hither and thither, barking up a storm. The members of the hunt have no previous knowledge of where the drag rider went, so the mystery remains."

"No death. No tormenting of small animals," Jay finished.

"Excellent! Not traditional, but still exciting. That's a wonderful solution, ladies," Ethne complimented. "It's a shame Brendan will never agree to it."

Luci and Jay walked back to River House dejected.

"We gave it our best shot. Maybe Glin will have been able to convince Brendan," Jay remarked with as much hope as she could muster.

"Maybe Logan was right. They've been doing this for hundreds of years; it's too much to expect change overnight."

"Change is always overnight, even if it takes years in the making," Jay pointed out.

"This might be the beginning of change."

"Sure."

From behind them came the sound of hooves on the driveway. They turned and saw Logan riding Balar. He gave them a small wave and trotted past.

"Would Logan be satisfied with a drag hunt?" Jay asked.

"Probably not."

"Well, everyone on the hunt is just like Logan."

Luci sighed as they walked up to the front door and entered River House.

They found Stacey in the library, still on the phone, with Daria nearby reading a horse magazine.

"Who's she talking to now?" Jay whispered.

"Some newspaper in Dublin, I think."

"Did Glin come back?"

Daria shook her head. "I haven't seen him. But Fran's been looking for you."

"Are we in trouble again?" Luci moaned.

"I don't think so."

"Phew!"

As they began to leave the room Tess ran down the hall, scrambling around the corner and making a mad dash into the library. She was followed by Siobhan racing after her.

"Come back here, you little devil!"

Tess made a beeline for Stacey and immediately jumped up on her leg.

"Get away!" Stacey put her hand over the mouthpiece.

Tess wagged her tail so fast, it became a blur.

Siobhan reached down to grab her and Tess zipped under Stacey's chair.

Tess scampered to the sofa with Siobhan two steps behind. Daria leaped to her feet and tried to trap Tess before she made it under the furniture, but she was too late. Tess disappeared under the sofa. Daria got down on her stomach and tried to reach for the puppy.

"Hmm. Nothing's changed," Jay remarked as they headed back to their room.

"So what are we going to do about tomorrow? Do we go on the hunt or do we sit this dance out?" Luci asked as they entered the room.

Jay fell back onto her bed. "Ah. A real mattress once again." She paused. "I don't know what to do."

"Me neither."

There was a tap on their window and Luci looked up. Glin was standing outside and waved to her. Luci went to the sliding glass door and opened it.

"You finally made it back."

"Long story," he admitted.

"Well, don't stand out there," Jay said.

Glin paused.

"Come in just for a minute. You're going to get wet out there."

Glin looked to the right and left then stepped inside.

"So tell us. What happened?" Luci asked.

"I got to O'Rahilly's place. It's a large stable, very neat, everything's perfect."

"Figures," Jay commented.

"I greeted him. He recognized me, and then you'll never believe what happened next."

Jay sat up. "Don't keep us in suspense! What?"

"Logan rode up on that horse."

"Logan?" Luci gasped.

Glin nodded. "Don't tell anyone he did."

"Okay," Luci agreed.

"Why not?"

"He'll get embarrassed," Glin explained. "We laid it all out for Brendan, all the details."

"And . . ."

"And that was the end of it. He was very polite. He listened. We told him you were at Ethne's and stressed how deeply she felt about this issue."

"I guess we've done everything we can."

There was a knock on the door. "Luci. Jay. Are you home?"

"It's Fran!" Luci mouthed the words.

"Under the bed!"

"No! In the bathroom!" Luci grabbed Glin's arm and pulled him along.

"Let me go out the window," Glin whispered.

"Too late. She'll hear it." Luci pushed him in the bathroom and closed the door. She took a deep breath and opened the door to the hallway. "Hi."

Fran stepped inside. "What's up?"

"Nothing," Jay replied evenly.

Fran sat in the wooden chair. "Siobhan tells me we're the talk of Connemara."

"Terrific," Jay murmured.

"We've forced people to take sides in this issue."

"That'll make Stacey happy."

"This has never happened to me on a tour," Fran admitted.

"You're not calling the home office, are you?" Luci asked.

"No. It hasn't come to that. I *will* say that you are a very spirited group."

Jay smiled. "That's a good thing, isn't it?"

"Up to a point," Fran replied. "Have you decided if you're riding tomorrow?"

They both shook their heads.

"I'm going to ask everyone to refrain from making value judgments about attending the hunt tomorrow."

"Good idea," Luci remarked.

Was Fran ever going to leave or was she going to sleep in their room that night?

Jay stood. "Isn't it dinnertime? I'm starving."

"You sound like Daria." Fran laughed. "But you're right—it is time."

"I guess we should clean up. You want to use the bathroom first, Luci?"

Was Jay out of her mind? "No."

"Okay. I'll be out in a minute," Jay said as she opened the bathroom door and went in.

Luci held her breath.

Nothing happened.

Fran went to the hallway door. "See you at dinner."

Luci tried hard to smile. "Yeah. See you." Luci closed the door, slumped against it, and held her hand over her heart. It was pounding so hard it was nearly on the outside.

Jay poked her head out of the bathroom. "Did she leave?"

"Yes."

Glin pushed out of the bathroom and headed to the sliding doors. "You women are crazy!" He was out of the room and disappeared in a second.

Jay and Luci looked at each other for a moment and burst into laughter.

Chapter Nineteen

They were having dessert in the blue room. Siobhan had made Luci's favorite—apple pie with custard. She had promised to write down the recipe for her special brown bread and now gave it to Luci with a smile.

"Wheat meal?" Luci asked as she read the ingredients. "Is that whole wheat?"

Siobhan nodded.

"Fran . . ." Luci began.

Fran was about to leave the library. "Yes, we'll stop at a Quinnsworth before we leave the country."

Stacey shook her head. "I can't believe you'd carry flour back to America. We have it at home."

"This is Irish flour."

Stacey bit into an apple. "That's five extra pounds in your luggage."

"Um-hmm," Luci replied, studying the recipe.

"We're all set for tomorrow," Stacey told them after Fran and Siobhan left.

"Is CNN coming?" Daria asked.

"Dublin News will forward the tape."

Jay ate a bite of pie. "This will be a media event."

"Yes."

"Does Brendan know that? Isn't he being blind-sided?" Luci asked.

Stacey shook her head. "He saw the reporters last time. Glin spoke to him. He has to know something's up."

"I suppose," Jay said, not at all convinced.

They were silent for a moment.

"Maybe Ethne and Brendan will get back together after tomorrow," Aimee commented.

They all stared at her.

"They've been enemies for thirty years or more."

Aimee shrugged. "There was no communication. Now they'll talk."

Stacey stared at her in disbelief. "He threw her out of the pub. Should she forgive him?"

"He pushed her," Jay corrected.

"He humiliated her in public," Stacey replied.

Aimee was listening carefully. "She humiliated him in public by protesting for all the town to see. This is a karmic pattern between the two. But I don't see any damage that can't be undone quite easily once they begin speaking."

"Sure," Stacey said as she put her apple core on a plate.

"If they don't do it now, they'll just do it in the next lifetime," Aimee said.

"Do you really believe that, Aimee?" Luci asked.

"Yes."

"Are some people meant to be together?"

"As you understand it, yes."

Luci was confused. "How am I misunderstanding it?"

Jay gave her a firm nudge with her foot. It meant, Why did you ask?

"Souls agree to certain things before an incarnation. They may have loved each other in many lifetimes but never managed to quite work it out. They would agree to try again. That doesn't mean they must be together. They just have another opportunity. This is a chance for Brendan and Ethne to resolve an issue they've carried with them into this lifetime."

Jay sighed.

"How do you know if you have an agreement like this with another person?" Luci asked.

Aimee smiled. "You know. Even if it's on an unconscious level."

Glin stepped into the room. Luci looked up, startled. "Any dessert left?"

They all decided to turn in at a reasonable hour since it would be an early morning whether they were riding or not.

"Do you think Aimee knows what she's talking about?" Luci asked.

"No!" Jay replied across the dark room.

"Maybe you have a soul connection with Sam. That's why there's a bond between you that can't be broken."

"No!"

"Maybe you have an agreement with him on the soul level," Luci continued.

"We have one life. There's no before. You do the best you can then you're outta here."

"What happens then?"

"We find that part out afterward," Jay replied.

"It's a nicer story to think we go through lifetime after lifetime with the people we really love."

"It's a story," Jay insisted. "I believe in love. I want people who love each other to be together just as much as you do, but in the real world things keep them apart."

"That's why they need another lifetime."

"Good night, Luci."

Luci rolled over. "Good night."

She fell asleep wondering if she had ever met Glin before she was Lucienne Fortune McKennitt.

He was juggling colored spheres, but they hung in the air moving in slow motion. Eight? One for each color of the rainbow. Suddenly they burst into cascades of confetti.

The bed was shaking.

"Go away," Luci said.

The bed moved again.

"Jay. Stop it."

The rocking motion continued.

Luci woke. The bed was moving. She opened her eyes. Jay wasn't there. She held herself still. She wasn't moving. The bed was.

Her heart began to pound so hard she thought it could be heard all the way to New York. She was terrified. If she did nothing, would she be hurt? If she cried out, would she be hurt?

She had to do something!

"Jay! Help!"

Luci flung off the covers and leaped out of bed. "What?"

Luci scrambled to flip on light switch.

"Luci. What's wrong?"

"It's the ghost! The ghost is here!"

In one smooth motion, Jay jumped up on her bed. "Where?"

"It was at the end of the bed!" Luci made the pressing motion with her hands.

"Did it lie down beside you?"

"No! I would have died if it did that!"

Jay was pressed back against the wall. "Do you think it's still in here?"

"Does it need to open a door to leave?"

"I don't know what rules ghosts obey!"

"It's probably still in here."

"Then we should leave."

"I'm afraid to move. What if I bump into it?"

"Ick!"

There was a knock on the door. "Luci? Jay?"

"Help! The ghost has us trapped in here!" Luci shouted.

Fran opened the door and stepped inside. "I don't see anything. Where is it supposed to be?"

"It was there!" Luci pointed at her bed.

"Okay, come on. Let's get you out of here."

Luci didn't want to move.

"Quick. Quick."

Jay didn't want to move either.

Aimee appeared at the doorway. "Hi. What's going on?"

"The ghost's in here!" Luci replied.

"Luci, calm down," Fran said softly.

Aimee stepped into the room and went directly to the center. She closed her eyes and was silent for a moment. Then she pointed her right forefinger at the far corner of the room. "Okay. You can leave now."

"Are you sure?"

"Yes. I have it pinned down. Go."

Luci and Jay raced for the door and headed to the library, where they met the others coming down the stairs.

"Is it the ghost?" Daria asked, clearly upset.

"Yes," Jay replied.

"Let's settle down," Fran told them as she shepherded them into the library.

Siobhan rushed in, pulling her robe around her. "What's wrong?"

Stacey folded her arms. "Your resident ghost."

"We have to do something about this," Siobhan moaned. "This will ruin our business."

Logan slumped into a chair. "No such thing as ghosts."

"You weren't there!" Luci insisted. "I was! I felt it!"

"You were having a dream," Logan replied.

"Not of being on a boat on the ocean," Luci snapped.

Glin made a time-out sign with his hands. "Come on. Let's not make this worse."

"Someone has to be the voice of reason!" Logan declared.

Aimee stepped into the room. "Hi."

"Is it gone?" Luci asked.

Logan rolled his eyes.

"Yes. It left your room, but it's going down the hall."

Daria jumped back. "Get it away from me!"

Fran raised her hands. "People!"

Daria shivered. "Where can we hide?"

Aimee sat down and curled her legs up under her. "Nowhere. It can go anyplace it wants."

Fran gave her a hard look. "Aimee, don't add to the problem."

Aimee opened her eyes wide.

"She's the only one in contact with the thing!" Stacey pointed out.

Logan stood. "That's it. I'm going back to sleep." He left.

"I suggest we all do that," Fran said calmly.

"I don't think so," Stacey replied firmly.

Siobhan nodded. "We have to settle this."

There was silence.

"We could have a séance," Jay offered. "Maybe Aimee could talk to the ghost and make it vacate the premises."

"Yeah!" Daria agreed quickly.

Fran shook her head. "Let's keep our wits about us."

Luci looked to Aimee. "Can you contact this ghost?"

"I think so."

"Let's do it," Stacey said.

"Absolutely," Jay concurred.

They waited for Glin.

He shrugged. "If you believe it will help, I'm in."

"You don't have to do this, Fran," Luci told her. "It's probably better if nonbelievers don't."

Fran shook her head. "Fine. Just don't stay up all night long." She left the library.

Siobhan looked to Aimee. "Is there anything you need?"

"A white candle."

Siobhan went to the secretary, removed a white candle from a drawer, and exchanged it with a blue candle in a brass holder. "Here you are," she said as she placed it on the coffee table with some matches. "Good luck."

"Thanks," Aimee replied brightly.

Siobhan closed the library door as she left.

"What do we have to do?" Jay asked.

Aimee moved the candlestick to the middle of the table. "Turn off the lights and we'll all join hands. A circle is very powerful."

"Will it come in here and attack us?" Daria worried.

"No. We'll be safe," Aimee assured her as she lit the candle. "Focus on the flame."

Luci noticed Aimee was silently mouthing words.

Stacey shut the lights off and joined the circle.

Glin gave Luci's hand a firm squeeze.

Aimee took several deep breaths. "Goddess, we ask for your protection. We ask that you guide our efforts here for the highest good of all concerned." She took several more breaths and then there was a very long silence.

A slight breeze blew through the room; on it was the scent of roses. The flame wavered then straightened.

"Spirit of the house, come to us now," Aimee intoned.

Luci focused on the candle. The flame began to bend and curve even though there was no movement of air, spiraling upward, growing in length until it was nearly six inches long. Having never witnessed anything like that before, Luci stared at the candle in disbelief. Was it possible for a flame to turn itself into a corkscrew?

The scent of roses became so overpowering that it became difficult to breathe. Was it her imagination?

The flame sparked and sputtered. Something very strange was going on and Luci gripped Glin's hand tighter.

"Spirit of the house, why are you here?" Aimee asked.

It seemed as though someone had blown a cool breeze at the back of Luci's neck, making her hair stand on end. The flame danced above the candle.

"But you can't. You're upsetting everyone."

Luci couldn't help herself. She looked across the candle to the other side of the circle. Aimee had her eyes open, her face was relaxed, and her hair was standing on end, too. But then again, that's what it always did.

"Go into the light. You don't belong here."

Luci wondered if that was the light everyone talked about. The one that led from the Earth to the Great Beyond. Wasn't there supposed to be a guide waiting for everyone after they finished living? Had this ghost's guardian angel gotten lost?

"I understand that part, but you have to understand how these people feel. They're trying to run a business. You'll scare the customers away. . . . Okay . . . uh-huh . . . yeah. I don't think so."

Luci stared at Aimee. This had become like a telephone conversation.

"What do you want? . . . No, they won't agree to that. I can go talk to them, but they won't . . . Not on the first floor. I'm sure . . . Is there? Yeah? Yeah. Uh-huh. Down the hall and then left. Can I have your word on that? . . . I'm sure they'll agree. They're very nice."

Luci would have given a whole month's allowance to have heard the other side of the conversation. What was this ghost saying!

"All right. I'll tell them. Find peace. May the Goddess be with you."

An instant later the flame was extinguished and Daria screamed.

Stacey snapped on the light. "Well?"

Aimee tilted her head so far to the right it nearly touched her shoulder. Luci could hear the joints popping. "He's not going anywhere. This is his house and he's staying."

"That was a waste," Stacey replied. "Some exorcism. We would have done better calling Linda Blair."

Aimee tilted her head to the left and cracked the other side. "Not really. I negotiated a settlement. There's a room above the third floor and he's agreed to stay there if the MacNeasas keep the guests away."

"Since when do ghosts make demands?" Jay asked.

"Modern times have arrived," Glin replied. "Even in the afterlife."

"He's not ready to give the house up or go into the light. He was born here and died here, so he feels a proprietary right." Aimee stood up. "I think it's over now. Good night." She left the room.

Luci tried to collect her thoughts.

"It's over? Just like that?" Jay asked.

"I don't think she was talking to anyone," Daria said.

"What about the candle?"

"What about it?"

"Did you see the flame? It got this long!" Luci raised her hand to the ceiling.

"Did not," Daria replied.

"Were you looking at the flame?" Luci was amazed.

"Yes."

"You didn't see anything?"

"No."

"Did you smell the roses?"

"Oh please," Stacey groaned.

Luci looked to Jay. "It was like someone spilled a bottle of Tea Rose perfume in here."

Jay shook her head. "Sorry."

Luci turned her finger in a circle. "The flame nearly twisted itself into a knot." She looked to Glin.

He shook his head.

"It was just a flame," Stacey assured her.

"What about the breeze?"

They all shook their heads slowly.

Luci stood. "Yeah, okay, great. So I'm losing my mind. Since the ghost doesn't exist, I'm going to sleep." She walked from the room.

How was it possible no one else had smelled the roses? Maybe it was possible her eyes had played tricks on her, but her nose hadn't.

Luci walked down the hall. Maybe she was just tired. Maybe it was stress. Maybe it was low blood sugar.

Aimee came out of the kitchen carrying a plate with a sandwich on it and a glass of milk. "I saw it, too," she said, and kept walking down the hall.

Chapter Twenty

Luci woke and lay in bed wondering what she should do. If Stacey's plan worked, there was no reason not to ride on the hunt. If Brendan O'Rahilly didn't go along with it, Luci would be embarrassed to seem to support the abuse of animal rights, even in the minimal way hill-toppers did. Luci had never had to face such a complicated moral issue before and she wondered what her mother would have advised her to do.

Neither of her parents would want to see an animal hurt or used in any way. Her father's greatest violence to wildlife was picking the aphids off the tomato plants he raised on their tiny terrace. They even had a sonic mouse repeller rather than set out traps.

The small travel alarm sounded and Jay reached for it. "Luci, are you awake?"

"Yes."

"Have you decided what to do?"

"No, have you?"

"No."

"How long is it going to take us to make up our minds?"

"I wish we had a couple more years."

"Me, too."

Jay sat up in the bed and pulled her legs close to her. "Why don't we just stand by? We can't go far wrong that way. Of course that would mean disobeying Stacey's Eleventh Commandment."

"Right. Thou shalt not stand idly by." Luci thought about it for a moment. "Fine. We stay on the ground."

"Phew. I'm glad we figured that out. Can we go back to sleep since we don't have to dress?"

"Sounds good to me."

They snuggled back down under the covers. Luci became aware of voices in the hall.

"You can't do that!"

"I can do anything I want. This is a free country!"

"You'll ruin everything."

"You will."

There was a bang on their door.

"So much for sleeping," Jay grumbled as she got out of bed to open the door.

Stacey strode in wearing her riding clothes. "Are you two riding today?"

"No."

"Good. You'll just add to the confusion," Daria replied as she entered the room.

"What's this about?" Luci asked.

"We have to ride," Stacey said.

Luci tried to follow this conversation. "Why? I thought you were going to . . . ride the media."

"I can't do that. I'm an outsider. It'll look like I created a situation. We have to be in the field, away from the action. We let the cards fall where they may. All the groundwork's laid anyway."

Jay got back into bed. "Why don't we just stay here?"

"Why are you getting back in bed?"

"Because I'm tired."

"You can't stay here. Ethne needs our support."

"Does this never stop?" Luci groaned.

"You want to bail out on her now?" Stacey demanded.

"No."

"Then get up. We don't have much time."

Luci crawled out of bed. "Is everyone else going?"

"Yes."

Jay sighed. "I can't face pulling on those boots."

"Did you get boot hooks?" Stacey asked.

"Hooks?"

Stacey furrowed her brow. "There are two loops on the inside of the boots. You use hooks to pull the boots on."

"Really?"

"I'll bring you mine," Stacey replied as she left their room.

An hour later they were in the stableyard, mounted and ready to hack to the center of town.

"I would really appreciate it if you wouldn't

inflame any situations," Fran told them as she got on her horse.

"Of course," Glin replied.

"We'll be out in the field with everyone else," Stacey said truthfully.

"You know by then the action will be over," Logan told her.

"I don't know any such thing. I have no idea what will happen."

Liam picked up his reins. "I never suspected having guests would be so complicated. I thought they would just come stay with us and behave themselves."

"We'll have to write a manual for other unsuspecting couples who dream of starting an inn." Siobhan laughed.

"The pitfalls and the pratfalls," Fran teased.

"Exactly."

They began to move off down the driveway.

The sun hadn't yet risen, but the sky was growing lighter by the minute. The weather was what they'd come to expect. Misty. Soft. But this morning Luci was prepared for it. She had worn two T-shirts under her riding shirt and was toasty warm. Unless it started to pour, she'd be very comfortable.

Luci couldn't help but wonder what the scene would be like in the town square. Would there be a media circus or would the reporters stay away because it was such a small story? Would someone take their photos? Would their faces be plastered on newspapers worldwide? The thought of it made her cringe inwardly. She might want to be famous but certainly not for instigating a riot in a peaceful Irish village.

"Yo, Luci," Glin called to her.

"What?"

"You're a million miles away."

"No," she admitted. "Only about one mile."

"Are you worried?"

"Yes, a little."

"Don't be. These things are never as bad as the press makes them out to be."

Luci smiled. "That's right. You and Logan were arrested in Vermont."

Logan turned in the saddle. "It wasn't my fault. I was minding my own business when that Deadhead pushed into me."

Jay nodded. "What if we get arrested?"

"My parents wouldn't be happy at all," Luci admitted. "They're not like your mother, Glin, who understood political activism and served you hot soup as a reward afterward. My parents would feed me bread and water for the next six years, probably pushed through a small opening cut into my door."

"They would understand," Glin assured her.

Luci doubted it.

They walked the horses around a bend in the road and the town came into view. It was nothing like the first morning they had attended the hunt. The street was filled with vehicles. There were cars and vans and trucks as well as people crowding the sidewalks. Horses and riders struggled to make their way from their horse boxes.

"Oh brother," Logan grumbled. "It's a zoo."

Stacey pulled herself up straighter in the saddle.

"No change is without pain," Aimee said.

Luci leaned over to Jay. "Can we go home now? Would we be missed?"

"Get your horse to walk real slow and we'll hang back," Jay agreed.

Liam turned to the group. "Come along. Keep together."

Foiled.

They rode by the fountain in the center of the square, avoiding the person holding the boom microphone and the huge portable-lights setup. A reporter was already conducting a sound check.

Ethne drove up in her Rover and parked. She waved to them as she got out. In a moment she was surrounded by reporters.

"Do you really think we did her a favor?" Luci asked.

Glin nodded. "I do."

Luci looked at him and could see he was sincere.

Stacey drifted away and was leaning over to speak with a reporter.

Fran glanced around the square. "Stacey did all this?"

"Yes," Luci said. "She did it all alone."

"Then she has a real talent for public relations," Siobhan admitted. "This town has never seen so many visitors."

"Can't hurt a bit," Liam replied heartily. "Put this town on the map. Some publicity will help our business."

"There's no such thing as bad publicity," Fran added.

Suddenly there was a hush in the square. People stopped talking, froze where they were. The group looked around and realized Brendan O'Rahilly had ridden his horse onto the street. A priest came forward to him.

"What's going on?"

"The blessing of the hounds," Logan said softly.

Reporters began to move to Brendan as he spoke to a member of his hunt staff. Ethne stood still, eyes on Brendan, waiting to see what happened next.

The reporters crushed toward Brendan and he held up his hand.

"The tradition of hunting goes back to the earliest days of Ireland. It is a great tradition and one I am proud of," Brendan began.

Reporters began taking notes, the click of cameras was audible, microphones were held out.

"But times change. Do we change with them or do we retain the traditions we love?"

Luci glanced away from Brendan to Ethne. It was as though he was speaking directly to her. It was as though there was no one else in town.

Brendan shifted in his saddle. "People have come to me lobbying for changes in the way this hunt operates. Most of the members resist these suggestions. It's very difficult to part with something you love so deeply."

There was a slight murmur through the crowd.

Luci was holding her breath. What was he going to say?

"It's for that reason this change is necessary. We run the risk of losing what we cherish if we do not bend."

Ethne began walking toward him.

"From this day forward, the Connemara Blazers will be a drag hunt. It will be green, as some say. Earth friendly."

Ethne stopped next to his horse and looked up at him. She reached her hand to him and he reached his to hers. In the middle, their hands met and they clasped together.

Aimee cleared her throat. "Karmic pattern resolved."

There was a cheer from portions of the crowd, including some of the riders.

A smile spread across Brendan's face. Ethne was beaming.

"Let's have the blessing of the hounds and enjoy the hunt. You're all invited to breakfast after the ride!" Brendan called out.

Another cheer followed with applause and whistles.

Luci felt tears coming to her eyes. "It's so beautiful."

Glin reached over and patted Luci's knee.

"Okay, okay," Logan said impatiently. "Let's get on with the ride!"

Stacey shook her head.

"A real romantic," Fran commented as she dabbed her eyes with a tissue.

"We did our good deed," Logan replied.

Luci nodded. It had worked out. Maybe it was karma. Maybe people were meant to be together. She looked at Glin and smiled. Whatever it was, it was good.

SUMMER '96...LIVE THE 3-D VIRTUAL ADVENTURE!

T-2 TERMINATOR-2 3-D ™

UNIVERSAL STUDIOS FLORIDA®

For more information call (407) 363-8000 or visit our web site at http://www.usf.com